ATOMIC REX

WRATH OF THE POLAR YETI

MATTHEW DENNION

SEVERED PRESS
HOBART TASMANIA

ATOMIC REX: WRATH OF THE POLAR YETI

Author's note – The following story serves as a sequel to two of my previous novels Atomic Rex and Polar Yeti. I would like to thank the many fans who suggested that I bring these two monsters together.

This story was written with fond memories of Toho's 1962 classic kaiju film and with high hopes regarding the Legendary rematch scheduled for 2020.

PROLOGUE

ANTARCTICA: TWO YEARS AGO

Dark clouds were beginning to form over the valley and with them came a cold wind down from the mountains. The prehistoric beasts that inhabited the valley did not experience many winter storms. Typically, the amount of precipitation that fell in Antarctica annually was less than a few inches due to the limited amount of evaporation that occurred on the frozen continent.

Even when there was enough moisture in the air to create a snowstorm, most of the time, the tightly packed tall mountains that surrounded the valley shielded it from the worst effects of the snowfall. Most storms would form out over the ocean then move inland. The clouds were often too heavy to clear the peaks of the great mountains, and as a result, most of the snow would fall outside of the valley rather than in it. There were the rare occasions when a storm formed directly over the valley and unleashed a blizzard on the pre-historic beasts that inhabited its frozen plains.

A storm like the one that was currently forming over the valley would cause the animals in it to go into a near feeding frenzy. The herbivores of the valley were well aware that several feet of snow would soon fall over the grasses and mosses they relied on for food. That snow would quickly freeze into a near impenetrable sheet of ice that would cover their food supply, making it very difficult to feed for the next several months. Most of the grasses and mosses that the herbivores ate grew at the base of the mountains that lined the valley. The plant life managed to maintain a foothold at the base of the mountains due to the volcanic vents that ran through the mountain range.

A large bull mammoth was leading his herd to the side of the mountain to graze on the thick grasses there before the ice covered it for months on end. When the mammoths reached an area that was rife with grass, the herd huddled up into a tight circle with the adults forming the outer part of the circle and the infant mammoths grazing safely inside the ring formed by their parents. The large bull kept his large ears at attention as he ate. There was a cave on the side of the mountain above them, and some of the predators in the valley would use caves like this one to ambush their prey.

The mammoths were one of the biggest and heaviest animals in the valley. In the time before a storm, it was possible that a pride of saber-toothed cats might try to attack them, but the felines would need to be desperate to attempt such an attack. More than likely, if there were any saber-toothed cats in the area, they would opt to find easier prey rather than attack the herd. There was only one type of creature that the mammoths needed to fear, and as they were grazing, those very creatures were watching them from the cave above.

Several sets of pitch black eyes looked down at the mammoths from the cave as the pachyderms nervously grazed. One of the sets of eyes shifted forward as their owner prepared to run out of the cave and attack the mammoths. He was stopped as a large clawed hand reached out and grabbed his shoulder. The young yeti turned around to see the huge form of the alpha male yeti pulling him backward. The juvenile was hungry, but when he saw the thick muscles protruding out from the alpha males white fur, his hunger was overtaken by fear. Even at twenty feet tall, the juvenile was a good six to seven feet shorter than the alpha.

There was a soft grunting sound as the alpha male commanded the younger beast to be patient and return to the back of the cave with the rest of his family. The alpha was an old hunter, and he knew exactly when the best time to attack the herd would be. When the alpha had seen the clouds forming overhead, and when he felt the air getting heavy, he knew that the snow was coming. The alpha then led his family on a search to find an area where they would find abundant prey. When the alpha saw the grassy field and the cave above it, he knew that it would only be a matter of time before the mammoths came here to feed. He also knew that the best time to attack the mammoths would be after they had fed for a long time. With their bellies full, the mammoths would be tired and sluggish. The alpha looked down at the mammoths, and when he opened his mouth, a long strand of saliva dripped off his sharp fangs. Like the juvenile, the alpha was hungry, and he wanted to attack the mammoths, but he knew that he needed to bide his time if this hunt was to be successful. The alpha turned around to see the nearly twenty other yetis that were depending on him to feed and protect them. Many of the yetis were his mates and children, respectively. The alpha yeti was hungry, but his desire to provide for his family outweighed his hunger for the time being. The alpha yeti turned his head back toward the mammoths. He snarled quietly at the herd then sat down near the mouth of the cave as the mammoths gorged themselves.

After watching the mammoths feed for over an hour, the alpha yeti stood up. He roared and alerted his family that the time had come to attack. The alpha yeti ran down the side of the snowy slope directly at the bull mammoth who was the leader of the herd. The alpha yeti's family followed his lead, sprinting directly for the head mammoth. When the head mammoth saw the yetis coming at his herd with speed that they would be unable to escape from, the bull lowered his head, stamped his foot, and trumpeted a warning to both his herd and the yetis. The alpha yeti responded to the trumpeting with a roar of his own as he continued to run directly at the lead mammoth. The mammoth swung his tusks at the alpha yeti, and to the pachyderm's surprise, the alpha yeti caught the tusks in his claws. Then in a show of incredible strength, the alpha yeti pulled the big bull mammoth out of the circle that the pachyderms had created. When he pulled the lead bull out of the circle, the other mammoths panicked and stampeded away from the slope of the mountain. The stamped left the sides of the bull mammoth unprotected. The alpha yeti held the large bull in place as the other members of his family tore the mammoth apart from the sides. The stampede also left several of the calves unprotected by their elders. The yetis were able to grab three of the calves and kill them before they had the chance to catch up with the rest of the herd. The large bull was quickly bleeding to death, and the last thing that he saw was the jaws of the alpha yeti coming toward his face.

The family of yetis was just starting to devour the remains of the big bull when they heard a sound the likes of which had never echoed across their frozen valley. The sound was a roar that was louder and more powerful than even the roar of the alpha yeti himself. The roar came from the mountains to their left behind which was the great ocean.

The yetis looked toward the top of the mountain, and at first, their minds were unable to process what their eyes were showing them. It looked as if the top of the mountain had come to life and was quickly moving down the slope toward them. The yetis were still staring at the strange phenomenon when the moving mountaintop roared again. The alpha yeti stepped forward and sniffed the air. He shook his head in disgust at the scent that was coming from the moving mountain. The smell coming off the moving mountaintop burned the alpha yeti's nostrils. It was almost as if the scent of the thing was poisonous.

The rest of the alpha's family were shaking their heads in disgust at the noxious odor when the moving mountaintop began to pick up speed. The alpha could then see that what he thought was a moving mountaintop was actually a massive living creature. The colossal beast walked on four legs and was covered in light brown scales. The monster's face was flat and it had thick bony protrusion on top of it that formed a club-like knob. The creature's back had bony protrusions that sprouted out at irregular angles like the needles of a cactus. Behind the creature, was a huge tail that ended in a scorpion-like stinger. The monster's front and rear feet ended in long curved claws.

The beast was over fifty feet tall and well over one hundred feet long. The creature was a kaiju that was created by man when they tested their nuclear weapons on an island that held prehistoric animals who have roamed the earth far longer than the beasts of the frozen valley.

Before the time of man had ended, the people of South America had dubbed the spiked creature Armorsaur. The kaiju had destroyed most of Brazil, but when he found that the territories that surrounded him were occupied by other kaiju, he entered the ocean in search of new hunting grounds. Armorsaur would swim south to Antarctica where he would find a new hunting ground inside of the valley of the yetis. Within minutes of climbing over the mountain, Armorsaur had reached the confused yetis. Even to the twenty plus foot tall yetis, Armorsaur was a giant. The kaiju roared once more, and then he charged the gathered yetis.

The alpha yeti roared back at the advancing kaiju. The alpha yeti had never known defeat at the hands of an opponent. His might was unchallenged by all who lived in the frozen valley. The alpha yeti darted toward the oncoming kaiju, and as he ran, his family followed him.

The alpha yeti ran beneath Armorsaur's opened jaws and directly at the kaiju's bone-plated leg. The leg of the kaiju alone was more than twice the size of the alpha yeti. The alpha yeti roared at that living monolith of bone and muscle before him. Then he struck the leg with enough force to crush the skull of a mammoth. Despite the power and fury of the alpha yeti, the much larger Armorsaur continued to walk forward as if he did not notice the yeti's blow.

The alpha yeti watched as Armorsaur closed his jaws on one of his mates and swallowed her in a single bite. With a single swipe of his foreclaw, Armorsaur gutted two more of the outmatched yetis. After seeing several of their family members slain, the yetis, who were still standing in front of Armorsaur, turned and ran. The alpha yeti was still standing next to the kaiju's leg when he heard a crackling sound coming from above him. The alpha yeti looked up to see that Armorsaur had lifted his scorpion tail above his head. The alpha yeti could see what looked like a ball of lightning building on Armorsaur's stinger. A moment later, the lightning streaked out from the stinger and cut most of the retreating yetis in half. Roughly a half dozen yetis were still fleeing from the kaiju when Armorsaur took a few steps forward then brought his claw down on the primates, crushing them into a pulp. The alpha yeti watched in horror as the kaiju licked up the remains of what had been his family from the ice and snow.

Enraged at the death of his family, the alpha yeti charged at the hind leg of Armorsaur. The yeti repeatedly pounded on the thick bone covering that enveloped the kaiju's leg while howling in both anger and anguish. The skin on the alpha yeti's hand began to peel away from striking the plated leg of the kaiju, and all the while, Armorsaur continued to feast on the remains of his family. The alpha yeti saw the kaiju bend its head down and grab the bodies of one of his children in his teeth. The alpha yeti screamed again then he doubled his efforts at attacking the kaiju's leg. Finally, after repeatedly striking the same spot on the kaiju, the alpha yeti succeeded in cracking the kaiju's armor. The alpha yeti dug his claws into the cracked armor, determined to reach the soft flesh below it and make the monster pay for exterminating his family. The alpha yeti ripped off a chunk of plate and tossed it aside. When he saw the flesh of the monster in front of him, the alpha yeti tore into it with his teeth and claws.

The alpha yeti's face and hands were burned as the kaiju's radioactive blood spurted out from the wound. The alpha yeti jumped away from the kaiju's leg and roared in pain. Over his own roar, he could hear the much louder roar of Armorsaur whose attention he had finally managed to gain. Armorsaur swiped his rear claw against the alpha yeti's chest, opening a huge wound that ran the length of his body. The former master of the frozen valley fell flat on his back with the gaping wound in his chest facing the kaiju's wounded leg. The dying alpha yeti was struck by one more wave of pain as Armorsaur's radioactive blood spurted into the gaping wound in the alpha yeti's chest. The yeti howled one last time before looking to his left to see another of his children being devoured by Armorsaur. Unable to watch the rest of his family being eaten, the alpha yeti looked to the sky just as the blizzard unleashed its fury. The last thing that the alpha yeti saw was a wall of white coming down from the sky at him.

CHAPTER 1

LAKE SUPERIOR: PRESENT DAY

A school of small rainbow trout was swimming through the murky depths of Lake Superior. The trout were swimming toward the lakebed, looking for food that had fallen to the bottom of the lake. The water became increasingly cooler and darker as the school made their way deeper into the water. The school had almost reached the bottom of the lake when their sensory organs suddenly activated their flight response. The fish realized that they had swum into the domain of an apex predator. The school quickly swam toward the warmer water above them as a living missile shot out from the darkness below.

A long streamlined body darted after the school of fish, and vicious jaws snapped shut just short of ensnaring the trout at the back of the school. The panicked trout continued to swim for their lives as bright yellow eyes the size beach balls came into view behind them. The predator swerved his tail as he picked up speed and began closing in on the school ahead of him. The beast reached the school of fish and opened his jaws to reveal razor sharp teeth the size of railroad spikes.

The creature was over forty feet long and weighed nearly seven tons. The predator was a mutated pike. Once in its lifetime, the fish had been a regular pike, but when the kaiju known as Dimetrasaurus had made its home in the Great Lakes, the radiation from the creature mutated much of the wildlife in the lakes causing them to grow into giant monsters. The colossal pike was one of the creatures that had experienced such a mutation. With another burst of speed, the giant pike once more exploded into the center of the school of fleeing trout. The pike was rabidly snapping its jaws shut on the trout when the pike's body sent the same flight or fight response through its nervous system that the trout had experienced when he attacked them. The pike shifted its head down to see a set of jaws wide enough to bite him in half streaking up from the bottom of the lake. The pike reacted with lightning quick reflexes, and he was able to move just enough to avoid the jaws that were coming for him but not the body that followed it.

Saurian teeth snapped shut just short of the pike's tail, but the powerful body that propelled the jaws were able to slam into the giant pike, sending the fish tumbling through the water. The body of a colossal theropod dinosaur with long powerful arms came into the view of the pike. The kaiju known as Atomic Rex steadied himself, and then he darted for the stunned mutant. When the giant pike saw Atomic Rex coming toward him, the fish's naturally aggressive nature took over. Despite the fact that Atomic Rex was nearly five times larger than him, the pike attacked the kaiju. The giant fish dug its spike-like teeth into Atomic Rex's arm, and then it shook its head from side to side so that its teeth worked like a saw cutting through the kaiju's left arm. A cloud of Atomic Rex's own blood wafted into his face and eyes, and the sight and smell of it only further enraged the ravenous kaiju.

The nuclear theropod had hunted the pike for too long to let his prey escape him again. Rather than trying to shake the pike loose, Atomic Rex reached over with his right claw and impaled the mutant right through the middle of his body. The pike was too focused on trying to attack Atomic Rex to realize that he was now trapped by the monster.

The mutant was still tearing at the kaiju's arm when Atomic Rex snapped his jaws shut on the fish just below its gills, tearing the creature in two. Atomic Rex swallowed the upper half of the creature as the pike's jaw released its grip on the kaiju's arm and drifted toward the bottom of the lake. The trout who had been fleeing from the giant mutant to avoid being eaten now darted after its falling head to eat the remains of the predator that was hunting them only a moment ago.

With his prey devoured, Atomic Rex swam to the surface of the lake. When the kaiju's head broke the surface of the water, he exhaled the air that was contained in his lungs and took a deep breath in, but uncharacteristically, the monster did not roar at his successful victory over the mutant pike.

Atomic Rex floated quietly on the surface of the lake as his eyes looked to the sky above him. The skies had once been full of giant mutant seagulls just as the lakes had been full of giant fish and the land full of various forms of giant insects and animals. Atomic Rex had no concept of time. He did not realize that it had been nearly fifteen years since he had slain not only Tortiraus but also all of the other True Kaiju in North America. The monster had claimed the territory from the Rocky Mountains to the Continental Shelf of the Atlantic Ocean as his own.

For the past fifteen years, this had proved an ideal situation for the kaiju. There were several nuclear reactors in that range to satiate his need for nuclear energy, and for the first ten years, there were plenty of mutants to feed him physically. Atomic Rex was the unquestioned master of his domain. There were no more True Kaiju to challenge his reign. None of the creatures who had first been turned into kaiju when nuclear tests were carried out on an island populated with dinosaurs remained on the continent. While the lack of other True Kaiju guaranteed Atomic Rex's dominance, it also ensured that his food supply would quickly dwindle.

The area that Atomic Rex now controlled had once been controlled by five other True Kaiju. The existence of these beasts altered the very food web of the continent. As the kaiju moved around their various territories, spreading their radiation, they caused other animals to grow into giant mutants. Tortiraus's occupation of the Gulf of Mexico had created a plethora of giant sea life that inhabited the entire Gulf Stream. By slaying the other True Kaiju, Atomic Rex had also inadvertently cut off his own food supply. The nuclear theropod gave off enough radiation to create some mutants, but as he patrolled his vast territory, burning off energy with each step, he was slowly eating more mutants than he was creating. Atomic Rex was also faced with the fact that giant mutants ate each other without giving off enough radiation to create more mutants in their wake. After ruling two-thirds of North America for fifteen years, Atomic Rex had run out of food. The giant pike that Atomic Rex had just devoured was the last mutant in the Great Lakes area.

Atomic Rex swam to the western shore of Lake Superior, and when he exited the water, he looked toward the setting sun and the mountains that it sank behind, signifying the western limit of his domain. Atomic Rex reared his head back and roared at the sun and the mountains that it was heading for. The nuclear theropod was determined to cross the mountains and find a new source of food rather than to die of starvation in a barren kingdom of his own making. Atomic Rex lowered his head and began the long walk toward the Rocky Mountains.

Thousands of feet in the air above Atomic Rex, the mech known as Steel Samurai 2.0 floated silently and hidden within a cloud. If Atomic Rex had seen the mech floating above him, the monster would have relentlessly pursued the giant robot until it landed. Fifteen years ago, it was Steel Samurai that had drawn Atomic Rex into the territories of the other kaiju with the purpose of using the nuclear theropod to destroy the other monsters. During the course of drawing Atomic Rex into other the monster's territories, the mech and the monster had battled several times, and it was during Atomic Rex's battle with the mighty Tortiraus that Steel Samurai drove his sword through Atomic Rex and nearly killed the mighty beast. The kaiju had not forgotten the pain that the mech had inflicted upon him, and if he saw the robot, Atomic Rex would have stopped at nothing to destroy it.

The plan to draw Atomic Rex into other kaiju's territory was devised by the mech's captain, Chris Myers. As he was enacting his plan, he came across the man-beast known as Ogre and a woman he had captured, who now was sitting next him as both his wife and co-pilot, Kate Myers. For all of Chris's virtues, it was Kate who was the braver and more intelligent of the two. Chris didn't resent his wife for this; instead, it was what he loved and admired about her. Without Kate, Chris would not have been able to have finished his mission and to have Atomic Rex destroy the other True Kaiju. Kate then helped in moving what remained of the human population in North America to the Pacific Northwest, an area that was relatively unaffected by kaiju and radiation. Once the people had arrived in their new settlement, they saw the natural leader that Kate was and they elected her as their new leader.

Kate quickly delegated roles to people and set up a town that revolved around fishing and farming. As she was setting up the new society, Chris and team of people who had once been engineers managed to use the remains of some of the other destroyed mechs to turn the heavily damaged Steel Samurai into

Steel Samurai 2.0. The mech was now composed of the remains of the mechs of two of Chris's fallen friends from the days during the kaiju war. The mech was now multi-colored and more streamlined than the previous version, allowing it to have increased maneuverability.

Chris looked over toward his wife, and he could see the stress on her face as she looked at the kaiju on her screen. He knew that with Atomic Rex heading west, she was not only worried about the people under her care, but for the lives of their son and daughter as well. Chris placed his hand on her shoulder. "This time, he is going to cross the mountains, isn't he?"

Kate nodded. "I think so. We have been keeping an eye on his food and radiation supply for some time. The reactors that we left for him are still giving off plenty of energy, but his food supply is almost totally exhausted. Our latest scans show that there are less than twenty mutants of kaiju-size proportions for him to feed on." She sighed. "He is going to go looking for more food. If he crosses the Rockies, he will smell the food at our settlement and head straight for it."

Kate looked over at her husband. "It's a good thing that we have been preparing for this eventuality." She took a deep breath. "We are going to have to engage Atomic Rex again. We are going to have to initiate Operation South America."

Chris nodded then he leaned over and kissed his wife. "Okay then. Let's get home and take care of things for the community and our kids, and then we can make sure that Atomic Rex won't be a problem for humanity ever again." Chris hit the throttle on Steel Samurai 2.0 and the mech quickly accelerated to Mach 3.

When Atomic Rex heard the sonic boom explode in the sky above him, he looked up. The monster did not see what had caused the loud sound, but in his mind, he recalled the only thing that he had ever encountered which created such a sound. The thought of the metal creature that had driven the sword though his chest appeared in Atomic Rex's mind. At the thought of the mech flying above him, Atomic Rex lifted his head and roared at the sky in anger. He then lowered his head and doubled his pace toward the Rocky Mountains.

CHAPTER 2

PERU

The horror was everywhere. At every turn, there were monsters attacking buildings, razing tanks, and battling with each other. To his left, he saw a giant crocodile tear the head off something that looked like it had once been some form of a mutated *deinonychus*. The crocodile swallowed the head, and then it turned on the rest of the body. To his right was a creature that looked like something that was part whale and part gorilla with a lion's mane wreathing its head, fighting against a giant Viking with a war hammer. He turned around to see a giant bird fighting a demon that looked as though it had crawled out of hell itself. Straight in front of him, two more creatures that had once been dinosaurs had clawed each other to the point that their skin and muscles hung from their bodies as if they were confetti rather than integral organs for survival. Despite these mortal wounds, the two monsters continued to fight each other. He looked down at his feet to see humans screaming in fear and fleeing. As he witnessed all of this carnage, he was overtaken by it.

He did not feel fear, revolution, or joy at the sight of the carnage, but he was struck by an overwhelming desire to join in with the destruction. He felt compelled to attack and destroy all that was before him. His instincts told him that he needed to assert his dominance over all that surrounded him by crushing everything that he saw. He looked down to see a massive sharpened blade in his hand, and he lifted it over his head to attack the people that were scurrying around his feet, when he felt a shock run through his system.

Giant eyes snapped open to see the forest around him. He heard a voice addressing him in Spanish, "Revenant, wake up! We have incoming! I repeat, there is a kaiju heading toward us and we need you to destroy it."

Revenant shook his head and he focused on Ruiz Delgado, the one person whom his primitive mind considered to be a friend. Ruiz shouted to Revenant, "Quickly, it approaches from the jungle."

Revenant looked to his left, and he picked up a thirty-foot piece of steel that had been shaped into a giant knife. To his right, he grabbed a massive axe. The axe was made from a huge tree with two huge pieces of steel attached to either side of it. The colossus stood up. Revenant towered over the jungle with the tallest trees in the forest barely reaching his deformed knees. Revenant had an overall humanoid appearance to his body. He had arms, legs, a torso, and a head, but none of them seemed to fit together. Revenant's arms were different in color and texture. His right arm was yellow and covered in scales while his right arm was gray and had a thick covering like the skin of a rhinoceros. His torso looked like the mid-section of a human male, but it was covered in thick brown fur. His right leg resembled the leg of theropod dinosaur like an *allosaurus*. It was covered in brown scales and bent at an ankle that formed just below the thigh before bending at a forty-five-degree angle, reaching the ground, and ending in claw with a retractable talon at end of it. The giant's left leg and foot maintained a human appearance, but the disparity between the two legs and feet caused the colossus to walk with an awkward limping gait. Along Revenant's short neck were a set of gills that allowed the giant to breathe underwater when necessary. His face was a mess of scarred and mutated flesh. Revenant's face looked like the face of a wax figurine which had been exposed to high temperatures and had partially melted.

Revenant's tale was one of heroism, sacrifice, and horror. When the war against the kaiju had first began, Roberto Franco was a Special Operations soldier for the Peruvian army. Roberto had no family and little personal connections, so when a multi-headed snake kaiju attacked Lima, Roberto was tasked with the dangerous mission of parachuting onto the kaiju, using an acetylene torch to pierce the monster's skin, and then placing explosives inside of the creature. Roberto had succeeded in his mission when one of the snake kaiju's heads whipped around and bit him. The monster's teeth went right through Roberto's abdomen and out of his back.

The monster was still shaking Roberto in his jaws when the explosives that he had had planted went off. Roberto saw the explosion go off, and then he saw a stream of the monster's blood come flying toward him. The last thing that Roberto remembered was him sliding off the monster's back and tail covered in its blood until he hit the ground. While the explosive has managed to pierce the monster's skin, it had done little damage to the kaiju and the snake creature left Lima in ruins.

Roberto's body was not found until several days later by a rescue team looking for survivors in the wake of the attack. When the rescue team found Roberto, the fact that he had survived was the least astounding aspect of his condition. The radioactive blood of the monster seemed to have changed Roberto. His body had grown to over ten feet tall, and his skin had taken on a pale grey color. Roberto barely had a pulse when the rescue team found him, and they considered ending his life on the spot instead of letting him continue to turn into some manner of monster. The rescue team leader sent footage of what they had found back to headquarters through cameras attached to their helmets. He was expecting to receive commands to euthanize the young soldier when a command call came over his receiver.

"This is General Mendoza. I want you to bring that man back to headquarters immediately." The rescue team abandoned their search and they brought Roberto back to their headquarters. Roberto's body was quickly given over to General Mendoza and his team of military scientists. The Peruvians had witnessed many things during the early days of the kaiju war. They had seen how the Americans had created giant robots to fight the kaiju, but they lacked the money and resources to replicate this process. They had also witnessed examples of how the kaiju who had come from the island had the effect of mutating animal life around them. When they saw these mutations, some of the greatest biologists in Peru began to wonder if this mutation process could be carried out on a human with the human still maintaining some aspect of his humanity. They had tried several times to initiate this process themselves by exposing mortally wounded soldiers to genetic materials gathered from the kaiju, but in each instance, the subjects died shortly after initial exposure.

When the military scientist came across Roberto's body, they knew they had found a subject that they could work with. As the war with the kaiju progressed, the Peruvian military proved just as futile at fighting off the kaiju as the rest of the world's armed forces. One by one, the cities of Peru fell to the monsters, but with each battle, they managed to gain blood and tissue samples from the attacking kaiju, and each sample they attained, they infused into Roberto's body. Slowly, the soldier's body began to grow and mutate, showing the traits of the different kaiju that it had assimilated. Over the course of several months, Roberto grew into the one-hundred and twenty-five foot tall kaiju man that he now was. Large metal rods were inserted into Roberto's heart and thousands of volts of electricity were sent into it. The shock awakened the giant, but the creature had suffered a major loss of cognitive functioning during the mutation process. It had no ability to speak and seemingly no recognition of his life as Roberto. The man-kaiju seemed to know that it was human, or at least human-like, and he understood how to follow commands. It seemed that even though Roberto's consciousness was gone, his training as a soldier remained. The creature retained a desire to protect people and to fight off threats; in addition to this, he also retained all of the hand-to-hand combat and close-range weapons training that Roberto had received over his years of training.

The creature that had once been Roberto Franco had been renamed Revenant. He was tasked with protecting what was left of the Peruvian people which amounted to a settlement of several thousand people who lived along the coastline. Ruiz Delgado was one of the scientist who had helped to create Revenant, and he saw his creation as his responsibility. Ruiz spent as much time as he could with Revenant, and whenever possible, he tried to be the one who informed Revenant of his missions. When the Peruvian government collapsed, General Mendoza assumed control of the people who were left in the country and he moved them to the shore. He also made sure that Revenant and his *handler,* as her referred to Ruiz, were also with him.

Currently, Ruiz was accompanying Revenant as the giant walked through the jungle to fight off another threat from a kaiju.

Revenant had walked roughly a mile when the kaiju came into view. The kaiju looked like a huge monitor lizard with the exception that it walked on two legs, and its front claws had mutated into hand-like appendages. The aspect of the Revenant's mind that still had remnants of his days as a soldier in it immediately activated at the sight of the mutant. He looked briefly at Ruiz then he turned his head in the direction of the camp. The giant felt a compulsion to protect these people. When he looked at the kaiju, he immediately recognized it as a threat to the people that he was supposed to protect and to his territory. Revenant held his weapons above his head, and he roared a challenge at the mutated lizard.

The kaiju hissed when it saw Revenant, then it ran at the colossus. Revenant held his weapons at his side, ready to strike the monster when it came into range, but he was surprised when the monster jumped at him and reached him sooner than he had anticipated. Revenant tumbled back and crashed into the ground with the kaiju landing on top of his chest. Revenant looked up to see the kaiju's mouth open with its teeth baring down on his head. Revenant quickly shifted his head to the side so that giant lizard bit into his shoulder and not his face. The colossus moaned in pain, and then he placed his hands on the kaiju's chest and pushed it off him. The kaiju had maintained his bite, and as he was pushed off Revenant, his teeth tore a chunk out of the giant's shoulder.

The giant lizard tumbled away from Revenant, and when it regained its feet, Revenant watched as the kaiju bent its head back and swallowed the piece of his shoulder whole. Revenant moved in to attack the beast, but the creature spun around and used his thick tail to strike him in the face. Revenant was knocked off balance, and the lizard monster took the opportunity to spring at the giant once again. This time, Revenant was expecting the lizard's jump, and he braced himself for it. The mutant monitor slammed into Revenant's midsection, and he managed to wrap his arms around the giant's waist, but he was unable to force Revenant to the ground. Revenant plunged his knife into the kaiju's back then brought his left knee crashing into the monster's face. The colossus then pulled his knife out of the reptile's back and took a step backward. The monitor kaiju reared up and hissed at Revenant again. In reply, Revenant lifted his saurian leg across his body and unsheathed the talon hidden within it. Revenant then swiped his leg toward the kaiju, and in doing so, he used his talon to cut deep into the kaiju's knee. The kaiju screamed in pain and threw his arms out at his sides. Seeing his adversary putting itself into a vulnerable position, Revenant's military training took over his mind and controlled his movements. Revenant swung his axe at the kaiju's right arm, slicing it off just above the elbow. Before the kaiju had a chance to react to the lost limb, Revenant plunged his knife into its throat. The monster was choking on its own blood, and the soldier inside of Revenant knew that the creature would die within a matter of minutes, but then something else inside of Revenant urged him to continue his attack. Images similar to those from his nightmare flashed into his mind.

Revenant threw his weapons aside, and he bit the monster in its bleeding neck. Revenant wrenched the mutant's neck from side to side as he tore out the creature's jugular. The dying kaiju fell to his knees. Revenant then grabbed the kaiju's head and tore it from its bloody neck. Revenant was about to start tearing the dead kaiju limb from limb when he heard Ruiz shouting behind him, "That's enough! He's dead."

Revenant turned around to see a look of horror on his friend's face at what he had done. Although Revenant was unable to speak, he still felt human emotions, and at this moment, he was overwhelmed with shame at losing control of himself. Revenant gestured toward the slain kaiju when Ruiz held up his hand. "We don't have time for that! Liopleviathan has been spotted offshore! We need to return to camp immediately while there is still a camp to go back to!"

CHAPTER 3

ANTARCTICA

After remaining closed for several years, two huge eyes snapped open and blinked several times as snow fell off of their eyelids and directly into their pupils. A massive hand reached up and wiped away the snow that the blinking was unable to clear. When the hand reached the face and cleared the eyes, the creature's nose immediately inhaled an odor that caused the beast to recoil and crawl away from the smell. After crawling for a few seconds, the alpha yeti stopped and looked around. He was confused by the scent that had assaulted his nostrils. The odor was similar to the acrid smell Armorsaur gave off, but somehow it smelled as if it had been mingled with his own scent. At recalling the battle with Armorsaur, the alpha yeti immediately reached for his chest and the wound the kaiju had given him. The primate was surprised to feel only a scar across his torso where there should have been a gaping wound.

The yeti stood up to better gain his bearings, and he was hit by a spell of vertigo as he rose to his feet. The beast shook his head to try and bring his vision into focus because he felt that he was somehow viewing things from a different perspective than he should have seen them. The yeti found that he was able to see vast amounts of the valley from where he was standing, and additionally, the caves that he often climbed the snowy sides of the mountains to reach now all seemed to either be below him or at his eye level. The confused yeti began walking toward the cave that he and his family had hid in prior to hunting the mammoths and battling with Armorsaur. When the Yeti reached the cave, he stretched his arm out and found that he was barely able to fit his hand into the cave that previously he had been able to fit his entire body into. The yeti backed away from the cave, and he started to search for any remaining members of his family. The monster walked through the snow, sniffing the air, trying to find any scent that smelled familiar.

After walking for several minutes, he caught the scent of what appeared to be Armorsaur combined with the scent of several of his family members coming from the side of the mountain where had first seen the reptilian kaiju. The yeti was nearly overwhelmed by the scents and sensations he was able to detect through his nose. The beast had always had a prodigious sense of smell, but whatever had happened to him seemed to have greatly enhanced his olfactory senses.

The yeti began to run toward the familiar scents at a speed that belied his fantastic size. Ahead in the distance, he could see a mound with what looked like the arms and legs of his family members sticking out of them. The yeti approached the foul-smelling mound that wreaked of the odor of Armorsaur while still having the faint odor of his family. The yeti could tell that the dung was old and that only the sub-zero temperatures of the valley had preserved it.

The yeti bent down to the mound and he reached into with his hand. When he pulled his hand out of the massive pile of dung, he found the seemingly tiny body parts of several of his family members. Despite its strangely diminutive size, the yeti saw the face of one of his sons looking back at him from the palm of his hand. The unmistakable sight of his son's face sent a wave of anguish surging through the yeti. He looked into the sky and howled at the death of his loved ones. The grief-stricken yeti waited for a moment to see if there was a reply from any of the remaining members of his family, but the air remained silent.

The devastated yeti looked down at his hand as his intelligent mind came to the grim realization that Armorsaur had devoured his entire family. A rage began to form in the yeti as his mind processed this information. He and his family had been hunters but never had they or any predator in the valley wiped out an entire family! The yeti's sorrow turned to rage as he looked down at the partially digested remains of his son. As he was looking at his hand, a white mist began to form around the dung that was now the tomb of his brothers, children, and mates. Within seconds of surrounding the dung, the white mist had frozen the excrement solid. The yeti dropped the dung then looked at his hands to see that the white mist was emanating from his palms. The yeti turned his hands over and back again to see the white mist still coming from his hands then slowly subsiding.

The creature was not as intelligent as a human, but his cognitive abilities were far beyond that of any chimpanzee or gorilla. The yeti understood that somehow he had changed. He realized that he had grown tremendously in size and that his hands had somehow acquired the ability to emit a cloud that was capable of freezing anything that he touched. As the yeti came to this realization, two compulsive thoughts entered his mind. The first thought was to somehow find a family to replace the one he had lost. The second thought was the realization that with his new size and powers, he was capable of tearing the kaiju who had slain his family limb from limb. The yeti became obsessed with finding and killing Armorsaur in order to ensure the safety of a new family while simultaneously avenging the loss of his previous ones.

The yeti sniffed his hands and the pieces of frozen dung that still clung to them. He then sniffed the air and found Armorsaur's scent. It seemed that kaiju had returned over the mountains from whence he came and likely headed back to the ocean. The kaiju roared and ran toward the mountain slope that led to the ocean. The slopes, that at his previous height of twenty-five feet would have proved impossible for him to scale, were a mere trifle for him to climb now that he was one hundred feet taller than he had previously been. Within fifteen minutes, the yeti had reached the top of the snow-covered mountain. He looked over at the vast ocean beyond it for the first time in his life. He had long been able to smell the salt water of the ocean, but he had never imagined what the great body of water looked like. The monster took the briefest moment to appreciate the grandeur of the spectacle that was the ocean. Then he recalled his determination to find and slay Armorsaur. The yeti sprinted down the side of the mountain as he continued to follow the scent of his prey.

The plains between the base of the mountains and the ocean were over thirty miles long. The sprinting giant was able to cover the distance in under forty minutes. As he came closer to the frozen beach, the yeti smelled not only the salt water of the ocean, but also a smell similar to that of Armorsaur but again with something else combined with it. The yeti hastened his pace toward the beach, eager to see if he had located the kaiju or something else that would lead him to his quarry. As he came closer to the beach, he could see hundreds of walruses laying around what looked like a small mountain. The yeti could detect the distorted scent of Armorsaur coming off the mountain and he roared it. To his surprise, the mountain rolled over, crushing dozen of the walruses which were not able to move fast enough to get out of its way. The head of a gargantuan walrus rose up from the mountain and warbled back at the yeti.

The yeti had never seen a walrus before, but his mind was able to comprehend what had happened to the strange animals he now beheld. The yeti could see that, like himself, the mutated walrus was an alpha male. The scent of Armorsaur on the creature also indicated that like himself the walrus had grown to his unnatural height as a result of contact with the spiked kaiju. After devouring most of the residents of the Antarctic Valley, Armorsaur stayed in the waters off the coast of the frozen content for nearly a year, and as a result of the radiation he gave off, much of the local marine life had mutated into giants and monsters. The giant walrus was one such creature. After the terror that was Armorsaur had departed, the natives who lived near the mountains of the hidden valley were left with the giant walrus living outside of their village. Like all walruses, the giant was highly territorial and he attacked all who approached the beach. By preventing the natives from reaching the beach, the giant walrus had cut the natives off from the ocean which they relied on for food. The natives had named the giant walrus Beach Master, and because of him, they were forced to flee to the west where without the mountains to provide them some protection from the Antarctic winds, living was even more difficult for them than it had been before.

The yeti stared at Beach Master as the mutated creature continued to challenge him. The yeti could see that the walrus was far larger than him. He could also see that due to the changes which had occurred to Beach Master, by trying to protect his family, he had inadvertently crushed several of them to death. Images of the yeti stepping on members of his own family and crushing them to death flooded his mind. For a brief moment, the yeti considered that if his family had survived, he may have been no different from Beach Master who was now his family's greatest protector and threat to them at the same time. The thought further enraged the yeti and fueled his determination to enter the ocean and continue his pursuit of Armorsaur. The yeti roared, and then he charged at the monster which was preventing him from accessing the ocean and carrying out his vengeance.

Beach Master wobbled forward, bellowing at the yeti as the thousands of walruses that had surrounded him started diving into the water. The yeti rammed his body into Beach Master, and he wrapped his arms around the walrus's torso. Despite the yeti's increased size and strength, Beach Master was still far stronger and heavier than he was. The giant walrus slammed his head into the yeti's shoulder and sent him tumbling to the ground. The yeti hit the ground and rolled avoiding Beach Master's tusks as the walrus brought them down in an attempt to gore him. The yeti quickly moved behind the walrus and jumped onto Beach Master's back. The yeti tried to dig his claws into the walrus's back, but even his razor sharp claws were unable to pierce Beach Master's thick hide.

Beach Master swung his head around and dug one of his tusks into the yeti's shoulder. The yeti howled in pain as Beach Master swung his head around and pulled the primate off his back. When the yeti's feet hit the ground, he crouched down in order to dislodge the tusk from his shoulder. Once more, the yeti was able to move away from Beach Master before the giant walrus was able to gore him. The yeti took a step back from the oncoming walrus and he studied his opponent. After seeing Beach Master attack several times, that yeti was quickly able to devise a way to defeat the creature. Beach Master moved toward the yeti, swinging his tusks at the primate. The yeti watched as the giant walrus approached him, timing the up and down movements of the tusk thrusts. When Beach Master's tusks reached the lowest point of their thrust, the yeti's claws shot out and grabbed them. The walrus tried to pull back, but the yeti's grip was too strong to break. The yeti pulled on Beach Master's tusks, and as he did so, he began to unleash the freezing power of his palms. A white mist enveloped Beach Master's tusks, and in under a minute, they were completely frozen solid. With one quick twist, the yeti broke off the frozen tusks as if they were brittle icicles hanging from the mouth of a cave. Beach Master bellowed in fear as the yeti jumped forward and wrapped his claws around the walrus's neck. Beach Master began moving forward and swinging his toothless head from side to side in an attempt to knock the yeti off him, but the yeti had his arms extended and locked in place. As Beach Master moved forward, he was able to push the lighter yeti backwards, but he was unable to dislodge the beast. Beach Master pushed the yeti nearly half a mile inland before his body began to weaken from lack of oxygen. The yeti maintained his grip as Beach Master slumped to the ground and for several more minutes after that until the giant walrus finally stopped breathing.

The yeti placed his huge foot on top of the slain giant, and he roared, proclaiming his victory to the world. With the first obstacle in his quest vanquished, the yeti strode into the frigid waves with his mind set on destroying Armorsaur and finding a new family. As he saw the thousands of walruses swimming around him who had once been under the rule of Beach Master, the yeti considered that when he found a new family, he would need to be careful with them unlike the massive beast that he had just vanquished. With that thought in mind, he dove forward and followed Armorsaur's scent toward South America.

CHAPTER 4

PERU

Revenant was a half mile away from the camp and still running through the jungle when he first stepped into the salt water that had been displaced from the ocean. The water was not deep, but considering how far into the jungle that water had traveled, it confirmed that Liopleviathan was closer to shore than he had been in months. At the sight of the water, Revenant lowered his head and pushed himself to run faster. Ruiz had drilled into his limited mind that if Liopleviathan ever made landfall, he would utterly destroy the campsite simply as a result of him leaving the ocean. If the kaiju actually attacked the campsite, then every human being within it would be slain, before the monster made his way inland and decimated the entire jungle. As Ruiz tried in vain to keep pace with Revenant, he recalled how the camp had first been made aware of Liopleviathan.

When the survivors from Peru and some of the neighboring countries had first moved to the edge of the jungle near the ocean, they had built their huts along the shoreline. For nearly a year, the members of the campsite were able to survive by fishing and hunting the occasional whale for food. It was shortly after their first year near the shore that Liopleviathan first made his presence known to the people of the camp. Five men were in a hollowed-out tree that they had made into a canoe, hunting a pod of humpback whales that had made its way near the shore. The men had learned that by using the techniques of early nineteenth century whalers, they could harpoon the whale, ride creature until it died, then with the help of other canoes, gather enough meat and fuel from the animal to sustain the campsite for months. Dozens of hungry people were watching from the shore as the canoe approached the whales, when it was suddenly pulled underwater as if a powerful current had formed beneath it. The confused onlookers watched as a colossal set of crocodilian jaws completely enveloped the whale as if it was a minnow. The people on shore screamed first at the sight of the massive creature and then at the wake it had created.

Despite the fact that the kaiju was more than one thousand feet off the shore, the wake it left was akin to a tsunami rushing toward the beach. The people who had been watching the hunt turned to run back toward the campsite, but they had only managed a few steps before the wave overtook them. Had the fleeing people reached the campsite, they would still have felt the power of Liopleviathan's movements. The campsite was situated several hundred feet from where the shoreline was during high tide. Still, even at that distance, the wave created by the monster rushed in and swept through the campsite, knocking down the grass and wood huts the campers had created and dragged them back out to sea along with dozens of people.

After the devastation of Liopleviathan's passing, General Mendoza and the other leaders of the camp met and discussed the impact the kaiju would have on their campsite in the future. Ruiz had done some quick calculations on the creature based on the amount of water it had displaced. He estimated that the creature was nearly seven hundred feet long and weighed nearly one thousand tons. Even to a creature the size of Revenant, the sea monster was gigantic. Ruiz surmised that the monster must one have been a liopleurodon that lived in the waters off the island where prehistoric beasts had been turned into kaiju by the nuclear tests conducted there. The liopleurodon would have been a colossal creature to begin with, but after it mutated, it was more comparable to the leviathan of the Bible than it was to any traditional kaiju, and so Ruiz christened the beast Liopleviathan.

Ruiz also hypothesized that the kaiju must swim in a pattern around the Pacific Ocean looking for whales, mutants, and kaiju to devour, as those were the only creatures capable of sustaining such a monster. Ruiz was certain that the monster would return, and simply as a result of his passing by the campsite, he would once again cause serious damage to the settlement.

Mendoza was faced with several problems. The first was that he needed to rebuild their entire campsite. After talking with Ruiz, it was decided that all of the huts in the campsite would need to be constructed on twelve-foot high stilts to help avoid the destruction created by the waves the beast created as he swam. Forty-foot-tall lookout towers were also established, and the remaining binoculars and flares that the campsite had salvaged from the old world were positioned up there. When the whale hunters were on the ocean, the lookouts would scan for Liopleviathan and fire their flares if they saw him in hopes that the hunters could return to land prior to the creature's passing.

The decision was also made that if Liopleviathan was sighted that Revenant would swim out and try to drive the monster back out into the ocean before it was able to come close enough to send another tsunami barreling toward the campsite. Ruiz was strongly opposed to this approach, and he pointed out that Liopleviathan was nearly seven times larger than even Revenant was. Mendoza replied that Revenant would face the same dangers in engaging Liopleviathan that the whale hunters did when hunting the humpbacks.

The true nature of the threat posed by Liopleviathan was discovered a year after his initial attack. A large mutant spider had been spotted nearly twenty miles south of the campsite. Revenant was dispatched to slay the mutant before it ventured to the close to the campsite and started attacking people. Revenant, Ruiz, and a small contingent of men from the campsite had spotted the mutant in the distance when what they thought was an earthquake struck. The entire ground shook then quickly stopped only to start shaking again. Ruiz realized what it was, and he gestured for Revenant and the others to crouch low beneath the tree canopy. The tremors continued for several more minutes, and they increased in intensity to the point where even the nearby giant spider began to dance around in fear of them. Revenant, Ruiz, and the others watched as the spider began to flee back into the jungle until suddenly the sun itself was blocked out from the sky. They watched in horror as Liopleviathan's jaws engulfed the spider. The giant kaiju took a brief look at the forest then he turned around and started heading back to the ocean.

With the knowledge that Liopleviathan was capable of coming ashore, the campsite's entire plan for dealing with the creature was forced to change. Even to the uncaring Mendoza, it was obvious that on land, Revenant would be little more than a snack to

Liopleviathan let alone a force capable of fighting off the monster. The people of the camp once more looked to Ruiz who was able to offer up the suggestion that most of the liopleurodons went extinct when ocean temperatures dropped. He suggested that scout teams be sent south to see if they could find an area near the tip of the continent where the water was too cold for Liopleviathan and where there were not too many other kaiju that claimed the area as their own.

The search party was led by Vincente Suarez. The party had set out four months ago with one of the camps two remaining portable ham radios, and they were checking in regularly so that the campsite knew they were still alive. They would reach the tip of the continent soon and see if there was any evidence that Liopleviathan had entered the cold waters there as part of his hunting pattern. Ruiz's mind was brought to the present when the water rushing toward him reached his waist and forced him to climb a tree in order to prevent himself from being pulled back into the ocean. When he reached the top of the tree, he could see Revenant still running toward the campsite.

By the time that Revenant had reached the campsite, the displaced ocean water had nearly cleared the twelve-foot poles that the people had built their huts on top off. Revenant could see Liopleviathan moving through the ocean in the distance. He planted his axe into the ground to prevent it from being swept into the ocean, then, with his knife in his hand, he ran into the water and dove beneath the waves.

The various kaiju that made up Revenant's body not only gave him the ability to breathe underwater but to see underwater as well. A clear membrane slid shut over Revenant's eyes blocking out the water but allowing him to see everything that was going on around him. The giant could see that Liopleviathan was chasing a pod of orcas. The monster's body undulated like a great eel as he moved through the water, snatching up the orcas two and three at a time. In their panicked state, the orcas were swimming directly for the beach in an attempt to escape the massive predator in the shallow waters. The poor creatures had no idea that Liopleviathan was amphibious, and their strategy would only ensure not only their doom but likely the campsite's destruction as well.

When he saw Liopleviathan in the water, the part of Revenant's mind that was at one time a human being and soldier knew that he was no match for the monster physically. What was left of the rational part of his mind was struggling with the kaiju aspects of his brain that were urging him to attack the creature who had invaded his territory and to rip its heart out. Images of a blood-filled ocean ran through Revenant's mind, but the human within the monster forced himself to focus on saving the people he was tasked with protecting. For a brief second, the human part of Revenant's mind was able to gain complete control over his body. Revenant opened his mouth and sucked in a large swell of ocean water. The water filled up sacs that were located along the sides of his body. One of the many adaptions that the aquatic kaiju that made up part of Revenant had granted him was the ability to fill these sacs with water and then to quickly expel them providing him with an underwater jet propulsion system similar to the system that squids use to escape from predators.

When the sacs were completely filled with water, Revenant looked ahead to see Liopleviathan still chasing two orcas as they made their way to shore. Revenant placed his knife flat in his mouth, and then he positioned his body so that he was swimming on a collision course with the orcas. Once he was properly positioned, he unleashed the water that he gathered along the sides of his body. Revenant shot through the water like a living torpedo, and when he reached the orcas, he grabbed one of the terrified creatures in each of his hands.

Revenant looked up at Liopleviathan to see a mouth filled with teeth the size of locomotives waiting to devour him. The giant lowered his head and shoulders so that he shot beneath the opened jaws of Liopleviathan. Liopleviathan's snapped shut just as Revenant dropped below their range. Revenant allowed the sacs along the sides of his body to empty themselves and to push him as far out into Pacific Ocean as possible. When his sacs had expelled all of the water that they had absorbed, he threw the orcas as far away from himself as possible. Revenant then let his body fall to the ocean floor. The kaiju-man looked up to see the massive form of Liopleviathan gliding overhead in pursuit of the orcas once again. As he stared at the underbelly of the beast, the kaiju instincts buried within Revenant's brain overwhelmed any rational thoughts that his human mind could muster. Revenant quickly refilled the sacs along his body with water as he grasped his knife in in his hand. When the sacs were partially filled, Revenant forced the water out of them, shooting his body through the water toward Liopleviathan.

Revenant slammed into the underside of Liopleviathan, and immediately, he began tearing into the creature with his knife, teeth, and toe talon. A river of warm blood poured out of the wound on Liopleviathan. The giant kaiju roared, and with one fast twist of his body, Liopleviathan was able to shake free the creature that was annoying him as he hunted. Revenant's body tumbled through the water, and he regained control of it just long enough to see Liopleviathan's tail inadvertently swing back and crash into him causing his world to go black.

The giant woke up with no concept of how long he been unconscious. He swam back to shore to see that the water had receded back into the ocean and the campsite had sustained virtually no damage as a result of Liopleviathan's appearance. Ruiz and other people were on the beach cheering for Revenant as he waded out of the water. Despite the cheers, Revenant still felt ashamed. The human part of Revenant's mind, damaged as it was, could feel that it was slowly slipping away. He had succeeded in diverting Liopleviathan away from the campsite, and he had saved all of these people. Still, he had also been overtaken by an impulse to kill and destroy. More specifically, he had been overtaken by the kaiju instincts within him. On some level, he was starting to realize that one day these desires would completely rule his actions. He was also vaguely aware that as his rational thoughts continued to dwindle that he would most likely not even be aware of the process as it continued to progress.

Revenant took one look over his shoulder back at the ocean to see that Liopleviathan had departed. For a brief moment, he considered if he was a more dangerous threat to the people of the campsite than the sea monster was. A pang of hunger shot through Revenant's stomach and any contemplative thoughts were pushed out of his mind for the final time.

CHAPTER 5

PACIFIC NORTHWEST: WHAT WAS ONCE WASHINGTON STATE

Chris opened the hatch to Steel Samurai 2.0, and he closed his eyes as he breathed in the fresh radiation-free air coming off the ocean. He looked over the water to see a flock of seagulls soaring over the waves. He turned his head to the left and looked over the vast forest of trees that surrounded their camp. It was the same sight that he had seen from the top of the Steel Samurai 2.0 for the last fifteen years. The sight of all that he beheld caused him to smile as he thought about how a little over a decade ago what was left of the North American population was reduced to a small settlement in the middle of the country that had become a wasteland. The people there were doing little more than simply waiting to die. That was before Chris decided to use Steel Samurai to change things. That was before Atomic Rex had wiped out all of the other True Kaiju on the continent. Most importantly, that was before he had met Kate. The woman who would give him a reason to fight against the monsters, the woman who would show him that love could still exist in this world, and the woman who would show him that love could grow in this world as she gave him two children. She was also the woman who showed him that rationality and compassion were still relevant factors in steering humanity through this new age as she led the people of their camp toward the future.

Chris heard Kate crawling up out of the hatch below him, and when he looked down at her, he smiled. She gave him a half-sarcastic smile back as she crawled out of the hatch and stood at the top of the mech with him. She shook her head as she looked at her husband. "After all of this time, the sight of this place still gets to you?"

Chris wrapped his arm around his wife's midsection and drew her closer to him. "Seeing this place makes me happy, but the sight of you sends me into a state of complete bliss." He kissed his wife, and she returned that gesture with all of the passion that he put into it.

When they pulled apart, Kate hugged her husband. "Being with of you still makes me feel like the girl who was trapped by a monster and saved by a knight in his giant suit of armor." She laughed. "Promise me that we will live a long life together. If you go before me, it's going to be hard to find someone to follow your act."

Chris laughed and kissed his wife. "I promise I will always be there for you no matter what monsters we have to face."

Kate shrugged. "It's not the monsters that worry me as much as it is the rest of the council. They are not going to want us to use Steel Samurai 2.0 to draw Atomic Rex into another kaiju-filled environment when we depend so heavily on the mech for food and water. They'll try to use that argument against me in a feeble attempt at a political power play." Kate shrugged. "They still think things like political posturing have a place in the world that we live in. I am going to have to convince them that we need to us the mech to draw Atomic Rex away from us."

Chris shrugged. "They don't have any choice. It's either draw Atomic Rex away from us before he reaches us, or watch the camp and everyone in it die after that monster crushes Steel Samurai 2.0." Chris looked down at the camp. "Can we at least see the kids for a few minutes before we call the council to session?"

Kate started climbing down the ladder of the giant mech. "We are not just going to see them, they are going with us to the council meeting. They haven't really seen how to address a situation like the one we are now facing with a kaiju who is more powerful than our mech." She looked back toward her husband for a brief moment. "You and I may always be together, but our kids will one day have to learn to survive and make critical decisions in this world. It's time they saw their mother convince a group of stubborn old men to act in the interest of the human race rather than just for themselves."

Chris smiled and shouted to his wife as she continued to climb down the ladder, "That's another one of the reasons that I love you! You are always thinking ahead!"

The campsite that Chris and Kate had established for the North American survivors was an old fishing town. The town had plenty of housing and supplies that the people were able to use to make fish a large part of their food supply. The nearby woods also provided fuel for heating their houses in the winter. Fifteen years after the death of the gluttonous Yokozuna, there was even some game returning to the woods which provide extra meat for the population. Under Kate's supervision, the camp had even managed to grow a few meager crops including corn, cabbage, and potatoes.

Most of the people lived in the center of town in abandon hotels and office buildings. There were plenty of houses available on the outskirts of town. but the people wanted to be as close to the protection of Steel Samurai 2.0 as possible. The True Kaiju had not been seen in more than a decade. In the first five years of the campsites existence, there was still the occasional giant mutant that would wander near the town. None of the mutants were powerful enough to challenge Steel Samurai 2.0. As such, Chris and his mech were able to dispose of the mutants fairly quickly.

Aside from the repairs made to the original Steel Samurai with the remains of the other original mechs, Chris and his team of engineers also had access to every military base and research centers in the western US. Steel Samurai 2.0 had a fully stocked arsenal of ammunition and weaponry. Chris had even raided the legendary Area 51, and while he did not find any of the rumored alien technology there that conspiracy theorists had spoken about for so many years, he did find the most advanced propulsion and stealth systems on the planet.

By infusing the mech with this technology, Steel Samurai 2.0 became the fastest vehicle the human race had ever created. The robot was also equipped with stealth technology that allowed it to be nearly indictable even to the kaiju. Toward the end of the kaiju war, the government started moving away from technology that shielded vehicles from radar, and they started looking for innovations that could shield the mechs from the senses of a kaiju. The upgrades were not completed in time for the kaiju war, but they were developed enough that Chris and his engineer team were able to finish the work on the projects and apply them to Steel Samurai 2.0. The current version of the legendary mech was able to cast a reflection of the scenery behind it across its body, making it virtually invisible. The mech was able to move around in virtually total silence, and none of its vents emitted an odor that any of the known kaiju were able to smell.

As Chris was following Kate and their children into the town hall, he could already hear how the town elders would use all of these factors to argue against Kate's plan. The town relied heavily on Steel Samurai, not just for kaiju protection, but also for fishing and for performing the desalination process that the town largely depended on for drinking water. Fifteen years ago, when Chris had initiated his plan to use Steel Samurai to have the kaiju wipe each other out, he knew that he was making himself a pariah amongst his people. Even when against all odds he had succeeded in disposing of all the kaiju in North America, the people of the campsite were still ready to crucify him for taking the mech and leaving them unprotected. He felt helpless before that angry mob until Kate stepped in front of him and used her way with words to show all of the people what he had done. In only a few brief minutes, he had gone from outcast to hero because of Kate. Even after they had learned that Atomic Rex had survived his last encounter with Steel Samurai, most people still viewed him as a hero. The only people who didn't see him as a hero were members of the Council of Elders.

The Council of Elders were the leaders of the original camp when the True Kaiju still ruled all of the continent. After Chris and Kate had eliminated most of the monsters and moved the camp to the west coast, Kate was elected the camp's leader. While she effectively served as the "President" of the campsite, the Council of Elders still worked as semi "Congress" that worked in conjunction with Kate to govern the camp. While Kate was popular enough to make decisions that the people would back without the council's approval, Kate still felt strongly that their approval was important. Whenever Chis asked her why she put up with them when she could do what she wanted to, she would reply that it wasn't her power that needed to be limited but the power of the position that she held. She insisted that she needed to keep an established council with real power, because one day after she was gone, the people might turn to a leader who was not as effective or as morally driven as she was. If that leader ever came into power, there would need to be a precedent that the council could challenge him.

Chris would always shrug and accept whatever she said. He was always a soldier at heart and he was best at following orders. Kate was a thinker with the foresight to lead people, and as he followed her into the ancient town hall, he had total faith in her that she would be able to convince the council that her South American plan was in the best interests of everyone in the town.

Chris sat down with his two children. His fifteen-year-old daughter Emily had her mother's beauty but her father's temperament. She had an athletic build with blonde hair and stunning blue eyes. Emily was brave and somewhat impulsive; thankfully, she also had her mother's intelligence to help guide her impulsive urges. In the world that Chris grew up in, she would have been a sophomore in high school, but in this post-apocalyptic world, she was practically an adult woman.

Emily had a small team that she was in charge of whose responsibility it was to track and document the location of any large mutants that happened to wander into the western United States. Emily and her team used a series of trucks and portable radio's to communicate the positions and habits of any mutants they found to each other and to the campsite.

The western US was fairly clear of giant mutants. The only known exceptions were a giant big-horned sheep called Ramrod that roamed the area formerly known as Death Valley and a massive hippopotamus that had settled down in the Rio Grande. Ramrod was assumed to have been a wild animal which had been exposed to radiation, and as a result, grew to a giant size. The hippopotamus was thought to be one of the animals from the Phoenix Zoo which was exposed to radiation, and when it turned into a kaiju, simply looked for the nearest body of water that could hold it and settled down there. The hippopotamus was given the name Behemoth by the people of the camp.

Both creatures stayed in their domain and seemed to present no threat to the camp. Still, Emily made sure that she kept tabs on the creatures and their behaviors. For the most part, Ramrod would simply run away if anything came near it. The giant hippopotamus still maintained its territorial instincts. Any stray mutants that made their way into the Rio Grande were immediately chased off or killed by Behemoth.

Chris's son, Kyle, had much more of his mother's personality than he did his father's. He was thirteen with a smaller build, black hair, and brown eyes. Chris could see that the young man was extremely intelligent. He studied everything and everyone around him, and he also had the ability to see how events would play themselves out. Kate saw the potential of their children, and as such, even at their relatively young ages, she assigned them key roles in the community.

Kyle was in charge of keeping track of the camp's supplies and of organizing an emergency response to not only the threat of kaiju and mutants but also to things such as earthquakes and floods.

Kate felt that both Emily and Kyle were going to be the future leaders of humanity. She felt that they needed to be in meeting like this to see their how their mother handled the mantle and responsibilities of leadership.

Kate walked over and quickly hugged and kissed each member of her family before walking toward the center of what was at one time a courthouse. The entire back half of the courthouse was packed with people waiting to hear Kate's plan. Rumors of Atomic Rex attacking quickly spread throughout the camp and people feared the worst.

Directly in front of Kate, sat the Council of Elders. The four members of the council sat in chairs facing what was at one time the judge's bench. The bench was reserved for Kate, but she felt that sitting on the bench was a communication to the council that she was above them in terms of decision-making power, and she did not want to convey that message. Kate always preferred to stand on the floor in front of the council so that they were literally on equal footing.

The council was composed of four old white men with long gray beards. They had been the unquestioned leaders of the previous camp before Kate's natural abilities pushed her into a position above them. While council members were intelligent enough to respect Kate's wisdom, they still resented her for possessing the power they thought should be theirs, and as such, sometimes they would try to block Kate's plans simply out of spite.

Kate walked in front of them and smiled politely. She had long ago figured out that being purposely adversarial with the council only infuriated them and delayed actions which would benefit the people of the camp. As much as Kate wanted to win a victory over them and shove it in their faces, she knew that wasn't her job. Her job was to make sure that decisions were made that helped ensure humanity would survive. The most effective way to accomplish that goal was to placate the council as much as possible in order to get them to agree to the actions that needed to be taken.

Kate began walking back and forth as she addressed the old men before her. "Esteemed members of the council. We are faced with a crisis the scope of which we have not had to contend with since the formation of this settlement." Kate stared directly into the eyes of the man whom she knew held the most sway over the other members of the council. "Atomic Rex has nearly exhausted the biological food supply that was in his area. He will soon cross the Rocky Mountains and start a search for more food. His acute sense of smell will allow him to zero in areas where there are stores of large food, and he will head directly to them. In short, he is coming here, and even with the upgrades that we have made to Steel Samurai 2.0, we are still powerless to defeat him." Kate waited a minute for her words to sink in with the council before she continued, "We can't stop him, but we can lead him away from us and into an area where he will have an ample food supply."

The lead council member didn't wait for Kate to lay out the rest of her plan. Rather, he jumped ahead of her in an attempt to disrupt her, "Can we assume that you are going to use Steel Samurai 2.0 to lead Atomic Rex in this new direction?"

Kate nodded. "Yes, the mech is the only vehicle that we have which is capable of gaining Atomic Rex's attention and being able to stay far ahead enough of the kaiju to keep from being destroyed."

The lead council member gave Kate a smug look. "If this plan were to be put into action, where exactly would you lead Atomic Rex, and why would you lead him there?"

Kate gestured to one of her assistants who walked over with a large map of Central and South America. Kate pointed toward the map. "Chris and I have flown Steel Samurai 2.0 over Central and South America on numerous occasions over the past ten years. Much like North America was prior to Chris drawing the kaiju into each other territories resulting in the death of all of the True Kaiju excluding Atomic Rex, Central and South America have numerous kaiju inhabiting it that are creating giant mutants on a regular basis." Kate took a breath before continuing, "With the kaiju creating new mutants, there will be a food supply capable of sustaining Atomic Rex in South America. If we were to lead him into Brazil, he should be able to settle down there and live in relative peace." Kate took out a marker and she began to draw on the map. "As we know, the kaiju are extremely territorial. If we draw Atomic Rex into these other kaiju territories, there is also the chance that one of these monsters will slay Atomic Rex which would also solve our problem of having to deal with him."

Kate had drawn ten different symbols on numerous spots on the map. When she was done, she gestured toward the map. "Through our scouting missions, we have determined that Central and South America have been divided into at least nine and maybe ten areas by the kaiju who live there." She pointed directly to the lines she had drawn between Guatemala and Costa Rica. "This area is controlled by a nightmarish creature that Chris and I have dubbed Slaughterhouse." She closed her eyes and fought off a mouthful of vomit that wanted to spring up from her throat at the thought of the creature. "Slaughterhouse appears to be three giant bull-like creatures that have been fused together resulting in the beast having three heads spread across its body as well as nearly a dozen legs protruding from various areas of its body. The creature's skin is torn, revealing muscle in some areas and other parts of the monster's body are torn right down to the bone. Reports out of this area at the start of the kaiju war are sketchy. We do not know if Slaughterhouse is a kaiju that was fused together from three unknown bovine species on the island where the other True Kaiju originate from, or if he is simply a large and powerful mutant."

Next, Kate gestured to the area of Costa Rica to Colombia. "The lower part of Central America is controlled by a massive white wolf with some primate attributes such as an opposable thumb. The Colombian government dubbed the kaiju El Lobo Blanco. El Lobo Blanco is from the island like the other True Kaiju. It was once a species of Dire Wolf that lived on the island. In addition to its size, the kaiju's white color and thumbs are likely mutations as a result of the nuclear testing conducted on the island. The kaiju also has a pack of mutant wolves who seem to have accepted the kaiju as their alpha. Each of these wolves is only about a quarter the size of El Lobo Blanco. We suspect that this pack was once normal wolves who have been mutated by regular exposure to the kaiju."

Kate moved on to the continent of South America itself. "What was once Colombia is ruled by a seven-headed massive snake that we have dubbed Anacondoid. The creature slithers his way through his territory, crushing anything that it comes across and swallowing it whole."

She moved her hand over to the country that was formerly Venezuela. "Venezuela is the territory of another of the confirmed True Kaiju. The creature known as Innsmouth seems to be part of a human-fish hybrid species that lived on the island with the dinosaurs and other animals who became the kaiju. The creature's body has a humanoid frame, but it is covered in fish-like scales. The beast walks on two legs, but he also has the ability to breathe underwater when necessary. The monster has a face like a piranha with a long fin sticking out of the top of his head. The people who named the creature were obviously fans of the horror writer H.P. Lovecraft as the name is a direct nod to one of his stories."

Kate moved along the east coast of the continent. "Northern Brazil is ruled by one of the confirmed True Kaiju known as Armorsaur. The monster was one of the last kaiju that was confirmed to have left the island prior to the loss of worldwide communications. The monster was last seen heading toward Antarctica." Kate paused for a brief moment, as for the first time, she considered what the information meant when combined with a story that her great aunt Dana had once told her. Kate pushed the thought aside and continued with her report on Armorsaur. "Armorsaur seems to be a mutated version of an *ankylosaurus*. His mutations include becoming a carnivore, growing claw-like appendages, and a scorpion-like tail that can emit blasts of energy."

Kate moved her hand to the bottom portion of Brazil "The southern half of Brazil is the territory of Styracadon. He is another True Kaiju who came from the island. He appears to have some of the traits of the *styracosaurus* with a large horn on his nose and a bony shield over his face that is also wreathed in horns. He is different from the *styracosaurus* in that he is a bipedal creature with fully developed arms and claws. Additionally, he has two large horns protruding out of his shoulder blades."

Next, Kate gestured toward the center part of the continent. "Bolivia, Paraguay, Uruguay, and the northern parts of Argentina and Chile are patrolled by a giant dragonfly with tentacles instead of legs that we have dubbed Dragonus. The kaiju's top flight speeds are equal to if not greater than Steel Samurai 2.0. When Chris and I encountered this monster in Steel Samurai 2.0, we were unable to outrun or outmaneuver her. It was only by employing our stealth technology and waiting for the monster to pass us by that we were able to evade a direct confrontation with Dragonus."

Kate pointed to a marking that she had drawn over the lower portion of Argentina and Chile. "The southern parts of these countries are the territory of the largest land-based kaiju that we have yet to encounter." She winced at the term land-based kaiju, as she was still dreading talking to the panel about the kaiju that inhabited the equatorial portion of the Pacific Ocean. Kate composed herself then continued to describe the kaiju at hand. "The southern sections of these two countries are the domain of a two-headed, long-necked dinosaur. The creature stands over two hundred feet tall, and aside from having two heads, the creature resembles an *apatosaurus*. As such, the creature was named the creature Dipatosaurus." Kate took another deep breath before continuing, "Chris and I have also seen both of Dipatosaurus's heads spit out flames when it was attacking another monster." She paused for a moment to point to the northern part of Brazil. "If Atomic Rex is able to battle his way to northern Brazil and take the territory which currently belongs to Armorsaur, it is our belief that Dragonus, Dipatosaurus, and Atomic Rex will create enough mutants from the animals in the rainforest for the three creatures to have a sustainable food supply. If that happens, there would be no reason for Atomic Rex to head north as long as we move the nuclear reactors that we placed in the eastern United States to Brazil in order to ensure that the kaiju has an adequate supply of radiation."

Kate was taking a moment to compose herself before moving on to the more delicate topic of the last section of South America when once more the lead member of the council forced her hand. The old man stood up and spoke not only to Kate, but to the all of the people in the courthouse in an attempt to prey on their fears. "I notice that you have specifically skipped over what you and Captain Myers discovered in Peru?"

Kate stared at the old man. "I was just about to address Peru."

The old man cut her off, "I think that I can address the situation in Peru without having to take our mech into dangerous territory to do so." The old man turned away from Kate and spoke directly to the gathered people, "For several months, we have been picking up a series of radio transmissions from Peru." The old man paused for second as the murmur went through the crowd at the realization that there was another group of people still alive on the planet. He turned back toward Kate as he continued to fill in the general populous about the community in Peru. "Our Spanish interpreters have been able to deduce that these people are plagued by a sea monster they refer to as Liopleviathan. Mrs. Myers was correct when she stated that Dipatosaurus was the largest kaiju they have yet to discover on land, as Liopleviathan is over six hundred feet long and his very passing by the shore is said to send tsunamis barreling into the coastline of any land that it passes."

The crowd gasped at the thought of a kaiju more than four times the size of Atomic Rex. The old man had both Kate and the crowd exactly where he wanted them as he delivered the next piece of information that he possessed. "It seems these people also have a protector similar to our Steel Samurai 2.0. They have a giant that they fused the DNA of various kaiju into to create their own protector. They refer to this protector as Revenant."

After delivering all of this information, the old man finally posed a series of questions to Kate. "So the rough outline of your plan, consists of taking Steel Samurai 2.0, who is still the main source from which we gather our number one food supply from the ocean, who provides over forty percent of our drinking water through its desalination process, and our protector against giant mutants, and to use it to attack a kaiju who has already defeated the mech and nearly destroyed the last version of it?" Kate was about to answer the council and the people when the old man bombarded her with another series of questions. "There is also the matter of the monsters in South America anyone one of which could potentially destroy our most precious resource on this quest of yours." The crowd behind him was starting to talk louder at the thought of losing Steel Samurai 2.0 and all that the mech provided them. The old man smiled at Kate as he could see that the groundswell of support that she had in the camp was finally starting to erode. He continued his line of harsh questions, "What of this other camp and their kaiju-man? Have we tried to contact them? Do we know if they are friendly? Do we know that they won't try to attack us if they covet what we have? Have we even discussed with them if they would like having Atomic Rex dropped in their backyard?" The old man laughed a little. "Of course, this is all predicated on the idea that Atomic Rex is coming here and that we have to redirect him in the first place. Is it not just as likely that the monster passes us by and head to South America on his own or to some other part of the world?"

Kate glared at the old man. "In answer as to the direction Atomic Rex is currently heading, the last time that we observed the kaiju, he was heading directly for the Rocky Mountains. The kaiju are highly territorial and throughout their history have only moved into another kaiju's territory when provoked. The kaiju seem to have some sense of where other kaiju are located. Atomic Rex will likely head here in search of food first because there are no other kaiju in this area." She walked up closer to the council leader. "Atomic Rex is no fool. Like all living creatures, he will seek the path of least resistance unless coerced to do otherwise."

She then looked passed the council at the people of the camp who trusted her with their lives. "It is dangerous to risk Steel Samurai 2.0, but we have no other option when it comes to altering Atomic Rex's course but to use the mech. Our fishing fleet and desalination plants have grown over the past several years; we can still provide for the camp if the mech is gone for a few weeks. With the increased stealth and speed capabilities of Steel Samurai 2.0, there is every reason to think that we can draw the kaiju into South America without the robot sustaining heavy damage." She could see that her response was already helping to calm the people of the camp.

Kate turned to the council as she continued to answer the questions that she knew they would pose to her. "As for the group in Peru, the radio transmissions that they have sent out also indicate that they are looking to relocate because of the threat posed by Liopleviathan. If we were to use Atomic Rex to slay the kaiju in Central America and Colombia, the camp could relocate there. From that location, they may even be open to engaging in trade with us. Alternatively, if Atomic Rex is slain by one of the kaiju in the northern-most regions, we can offer these people the opportunity to relocate to the kaiju-free eastern part of the United states where again trade with them would be a possibility."

The people in the courtroom were whispering about what the possibility of trade meant for them in terms of increased food and resources. Kate looked to Chris. "My husband and I shall take Steel Samurai 2.0 and meet with this group prior to initiating our mission so that we do not simply lead the most powerful kaiju in North America to their doorstep without some warning. My husband has been prepping Steel Samurai 2.0 for this journey. We plan to meet with the camp in Peru and return to engage Atomic Rex before he makes his way through the Rocky Mountains and heads here." Kate kept her eyes on Chris who she was glad to see had understood her veiled message to him to go and quickly prep the mech for the trip.

She directed her attention to the council members. "This is all, of course, depending on the approval of the council. If the council does not feel that this is the most prudent and effective plan, I am open to further suggestions with the request that the council supplies an alternative plan within the hour to deal with the potential arrival of Atomic Rex." This time, it was Kate who pressed the issue with the council. "I respect the council's opinion that Atomic Rex may head in another direction, but I would suggest that it would be negligent of us not to at least have an emergency plan in place for the safety of our people." Kate stared at the council members as she waited for their response. The council members were ineffective debaters and leaders. They maintained their position of power simply because they were the leaders of the previous camp, and it gave the older members of the community some form of comfort and continuity to have them continue to be a part of camp leadership in some capacity.

Kate had hoped that one day the council would be composed of capable men and women who could work hand-in-hand with the camp leader to help the community reach its fullest potential. For now, Kate had to deal with these men and their jealousy. She knew that they would have to approve her plan because their argument had no substance to it. They had tried to make a power play against her by attacking her plan and by playing on the peoples' fears of losing their mech and the false hope that Atomic Rex would avoid them. The council members were still whispering among themselves when Kate pressed them for an answer, "Esteemed council members, time is of the essence. I must request that you give a ruling on the suggested plan to relocate Atomic Rex to South America!"

The lead council member scowled at Kate. "Mrs. Myers, you have the full support of the council in your suggested course of action."

A cheer arose from the people gathered in the courthouse. Kate turned and walked out of the courthouse, signaling for her children to follow her. As they were walking toward the towering figure of Steel Samurai 2.0 Kate's daughter, Emily, ran up next to her. "You and dad are heading to Peru as soon as Dad can get the mech ready, aren't you?"

Kate smiled at her daughter and son. "Yes, now listen to me carefully. This is not going to be the simple recon missions that your dad and I have flown before. This will be the most dangerous mission that we have undertaken since before you were born." She hugged her kids. "Dad and I love you, and it pains me to burden you with this responsibility, but there is no one else that I can trust here." Kate took a deep breath and spoke to her children with mixed emotions of pride and fear. "We need you two to keep the camp safe while we are gone. Emily, I need you and your team to set up a watch and early warning system for Atomic Rex." She placed her hand on Emily's shoulder. "Do not engage the kaiju! Just warn the camp if you see him." She then turned Kyle. "Kyle, I need you to start working on a plan to evacuate the camp and to move them to a safe location if Atomic Rex is sighted heading here."

Emily hugged her mother, "We love you too, Mom, and we understand. You raised us to be prepared for something like this and we won't let you down. What do you need us to do in case things don't work out?"

Kate looked to Kyle who she could already see working things out. He looked at his mother. "Excluding the mech, the fishing ships are our most important assets and our quickest modes of transportation. If we see Atomic Rex on the horizon, we need to have the ships ready to evacuate as many people as possible, and from there, we need to head north. There were never any confirmed reports of kaiju in northern Canada or Alaska. There is also plenty of snow and ice that we could melt for water if we needed to, in addition to hopefully non-contaminated natural water sources."

Emily walked over toward her mother. "I will position half of my team around the western base of the Rocky Mountains. If Atomic Rex makes his way over the mountains before you guys get back, we will make sure that Kyle and his team have plenty of time to evacuate the camp."

Kate hugged her children. "I love you, and I am so proud of you."

Chris came running over to his family. He tapped Kate on the shoulder. "The mech is nearly ready to go." He looked at his children, "Look kids…"

Emily cut him off, "It's alright, Dad, Mom already went over everything."

Chris smiled at her, and then he hugged both of his kids. "Well, I am going to say it anyway. I love you and I am proud of you." He held them for as long as he could, then when he released them, he turned to Kate and the two of them started running toward Steel

Samurai 2.0 with the future of mankind once more resting on their shoulders.

CHAPTER 6

ROCKY MOUNTAINS COLORADO

Atomic Rex stopped and sniffed the brisk mountain air. The kaiju's huge nasal cavity gave him the greatest sense of smell of any creature on the planet. Atomic Rex could track prey over a range of nearly one hundred miles on land and ever farther underwater. As the kaiju inhaled the cold air, his nostrils sent enough information for his mind to piece together a mental picture of everything around him in a fifty-mile radius. One of the most prevalent scents that the nuclear theropod was able to detect was the smell of death and radiation. The monster knew that somewhere nearby was the den of a giant creature that had been hunting in the area.

Atomic Rex had recharged himself at the long-abandoned Platteville Nuclear Power Plant, and while the kaiju's radiation needs had been met, his body still craved food. It had been two days since the kaiju had devoured the giant pike in the lake and his body was in desperate need of more meat. Atomic Rex studied the picture in his mind that the information from his nostrils had generated. The trail of death and bones led in a southwest direction. Atomic Rex growled and started to walk toward his target.

For roughly two hours, the kaiju continued to climb higher into the Rocky Mountains. As the kaiju continued to climb, he came across an ever-increasing trail of bones that continued to lead toward the summit of the mountain. The first bones that Atomic Rex came across were from smaller animals such as moose and cattle. The kaiju surmised that these were remains that had fallen out his prey's mouth in the process of eating and returning to his lair.

As Atomic Rex made his way closer to his prey's cave, he came across the larger remains of giant mutants. These were creatures that were too large for his prey to eat and carry at the same time.

The kaiju saw the remains of giant mutated bears and cougars spread across the ground before him. There was no meat left on the bones for the monster to scavenge, but the sight of the remains drove Atomic Rex's need to find food into a near frenzied state. The kaiju continued to follow both his nose and the trail of bones farther up the mountain until he came to a huge cave with the bones of giant mutants scattered all around its entrance. Atomic Rex was approaching the entrance to the cave when he heard a high-pitched screech and was simultaneously struck by a wall of sound that was so powerful, it knocked the nuclear theropod to the ground.

Atomic Rex rolled over and lifted himself back onto his feet to see two large hook-like appendages grabbed the side of the cave entrance. The hooks were attached to long leathery wings that were folded back over themselves to fit into the cave. The wings were followed by the head of a colossal bat with two long black horns protruding from between its ears. The bat pulled himself out of the cave and stood to his full height to reveal legs that were far too long for the creature. The creature's legs were more proportionate to a human than to the short legs of a typical bat. The bat's wingspan was over one hundred and thirty feet from wingtip to wingtip, and the monster stretched them to their fullest in an attempt to intimidate Atomic Rex.

The bat mutant looked at the nuclear theropod and screeched a challenge. Like Atomic Rex, the bat mutant's food supply was dwindling, and he saw the kaiju not simply as a threat to its territory, but also as a meal. The mutant screeched once more, and then he took to the sky.

The bat mutant began circling the kaiju in preparation for an attack. Atomic Rex stood up and roared at the flying horror above its head. The bat mutant replied by sending another supersonic scream at Atomic Rex that caused the kaiju to stumble from the sheer force of the sonic blast. With his opponent disoriented, the mutant dove at the monster. The bat's claws, teeth, and horns tore at the Atomic Rex like a whirlwind of razor blades. In a matter of few seconds, the bat was able to inflict dozens of cuts across the kaiju's head, neck, and back.

The bat was still tearing into Atomic Rex when the kaiju spun his head around and clamped his jaws down on the bat's left wing. Atomic Rex pulled down hard across his body, sending the bat crashing into the ground in front of him. The kaiju swiped his right claw across the bat's midsection, slicing it open. The nuclear theropod was swinging his left claw toward the mutant when the bat unleashed another sonic blast into the kaiju's face. The attack forced Atomic Rex to releases the bat's wing from his mouth and to back away from him.

The bat quickly flapped its wings and soared back into the sky away from the more physically powerful kaiju. The bat circled the sky above Atomic Rex, and once more, he fired another crushing sonic blast at the monster. Blood oozed from Atomic Rex's nose, ears, and eyes as a result of the attack. After stunning Atomic Rex, the bat dove directly at the kaiju's face.

Atomic Rex was far more intelligent than most of the other kaiju roaming the earth. He remembered that bat mutant's last attack, and this time, he was anticipating it. The mutant's claws were mere feet from Atomic Rex when the kaiju turned around so that instead of an exposed neck, the mutant was met with the most fearsome jaws walking the earth.

In a flash of fur, scales, teeth, and claws, the two monsters tore at each other. The bat was taking the worst of the exchange, and it was starting to pull away from Atomic Rex when the kaiju grabbed the mutant's legs. Atomic Rex pulled hard and sent the bat crashing into the ground. The bat had no sooner hit the ground than Atomic Rex lifted the mutant back into the air and slammed it back into the earth. Atomic Rex repeated the move several more times before the bat thrust its horned head at the kaiju's lower jaw. The bat's horns sliced open the skin underneath the monster's mouth, causing Atomic Rex to roar in pain and to release his grip on the bat's legs. The battered mutant stumbled away from Atomic Rex before once more leaping into the sky.

Atomic Rex could hear the bat circling above him. The monster was hungry and he was growing weary of the battle. Atomic Rex knew that the bat would try to stun him with his sonic blast as he had done prior to initiating his previous attacks. Atomic Rex dug his feet into the ground and braced for the attack while at the same time reaching deep into his very cells and calling forth the power stored within them.

The bat fired another sonic blast at Atomic Rex, and the kaiju weathered the assault as best he could. Thinking that he had stunned the monster, the bat swooped down toward the kaiju. As the bat was streaking toward Atomic Rex, he saw a bright blue light starting to emanate from the kaiju's back. The bat placed his claws on the nuclear theropod's neck at the precise moment that a dome of blue energy exploded from Atomic Rex. The kaiju's Atomic Wave continued to expand as it pushed the bat through surrounding trees and burned through his wings. When the Atomic Wave finally ran out of energy, it had leveled over three hundred feet of forest in a full three hundred and sixty-degree radius. At the edge of the blast radius, the bat mutant was laying on the ground with his wings completely incinerated and large portions of his skin burned off.

Atomic Rex began walking toward the dying mutant. When the kaiju had almost reached the bat, the mutant lifted his head and unleashed one final sonic blast in an attempt to save himself. Atomic Rex planted his feet firmly in the ground and lowered his head as he endured the bat's sonic attack for the final time. After the sonic attack had ended, Atomic Rex roared at the bat and walked over to it. The bat mutant lifted his head in a vain attempt to bite Atomic Rex. The nuclear theropod responded by side-stepping the bite attempt and latching his jaws around the bat's head below his horns. Atomic Rex planted his foot on the mutant's back, and the bat let out a meager scream as Atomic Rex pulled his head off of his body. The kaiju tossed the mutant's horned head aside, and then he began to devour what remained of the beast's body.

CHAPTER 7

PACIFIC OCEAN

Ice cold waves crashed against that giant yeti as he continued to make his way toward South America. His mind remained fixed on finding and destroying Armorsaur. Then finding a new family to replace the one the kaiju had taken from him. The monster had crossed half of the distance between Antarctica and the tip of South America. Despite the battle with Beach Master and the distance he had covered so far, the creature did not feel the least bit fatigued. The yeti had considerable stamina prior to the change that occurred to him, but it seemed the mutation he had undergone after being exposed to Armorsaur's blood had given him a seemingly limitless supply of energy.

The yeti continued to move his arms from stroke to powerful stroke as he continued to swim toward South America. He was unaware that below him, a mutated version of one of the deadliest predators in the ocean was stalking him. A body that had once been nine feet long had grown to a length of over one hundred feet in length after it was exposed to the radioactive blood of Armorsaur. Prior to its mutation, the sawfish was a member of the ray family that fed off small prey on the ocean floor using its saw-like snout to slice at small fish and to dig for clams. After its transformation and dramatic size increase, the mutant found that it needed to hunt larger prey. Shortly after its change in size, the giant sawfish swam up from the ocean floor to the surface where it used its saw to slice apart whales, orcas, seals, and large sharks prior to devouring them. When the sawfish detected the large form of the yeti swimming above him, the creature began pursuing the colossal primate.

The sawfish was swimming below the yeti for roughly a half an hour before it decided to attack the monster. The giant sawfish moved behind the yeti, and with a quick thrust of its head, the mutant's saw-like snout sliced into the yeti's left calf. The yeti roared in pain and reached down to grab his leg which caused him to start sinking. The yeti quickly let go of his leg and started treading water. The yeti was searching the ocean around him when the sawfish once again struck the primate's legs. The sawfish could see the bright white legs of the yeti kicking in the water in front of him. The hungry fish swam directly at its prey and drug its saw across the yeti's right thigh, slicing open the limb and sending a plume of blood cascading into the water.

Above the water, the yeti roared in pain a second time. The monster was intelligent enough to know that if he was to face the creature that was attacking him, he would have to dive beneath the waves. The bleeding yeti took a deep breath, and then he dove down into the depths of the Pacific Ocean. The yeti found himself looking into the nearly total darkness of the South Pacific. The only color that the yeti could see was a red cloud of his own blood that wafted up into his eyes and further obscured his vision. The yeti was slowly turning his body around in the water when he felt a sharp pain slice into his right hip. The yeti fought the urge to roar and expel all of his air. He looked to his right and saw a large mud-brown form dart past him before disappearing into the darkness. The yeti's lungs were ready to burst from their need for fresh oxygen, but the beast knew that the creature he was battling would soon be swimming toward him for another attack. The monster also knew that if he surfaced now, he would be defenseless against the sawfish. The yeti forced himself to stay underwater until he saw the mud-brown form of the sawfish streaking toward him again. At the sight of the attacking sea monster, the yeti expelled the air from his lungs, causing his body to quickly drop several dozen feet. The quick drop caused the sawfish to miss its target and swim over the yeti. When the yeti looked up and saw that he was dropping below the sawfish's range, the beast threw out his fist, striking the sawfish in the side and sending it tumbling through the water. With the sawfish temporarily stunned, the yeti quickly swam to the surface. When his head broke the surface of the water, the yeti inhaled several quick breaths of air before taking a long deep breath and once more plunging back into the ocean depths.

The yeti looked in the direction in which he had swatted the sawfish, and he could see the streaking from of the giant ray swimming toward him. The yeti waited until just before the sawfish was about to strike him, and then he shifted his body to the side. The sawfish was swimming past the yeti when the primate reached out and dug his claws into the sawfish's slimy body. The sawfish nearly bent its body in half as it swung its saw around and buried it in the yeti's left shoulder. The fish was shaking its head violently, causing its saw to dig deeper into the yeti's shoulder. The yeti reacted by pulling the ray closer its body and restricting its ability to move its head and cause further injury. With the sawfish caught in his grasp, the yeti once more swam to the surface to take a breath of life-sustaining air. After taking another breath, the yeti sank his teeth into the back of the sawfish and tore out a large chunk of flesh. The yeti spit out the chunk of meat as he and the sawfish fell back into the dark depths of the ocean. As the two monsters were sinking toward the bottom of the ocean, the sawfish continued to try to escape the yeti's grip while the yeti kept tearing out large chunks of the ray's body with his teeth.

The yeti could feel the pressure building in his ears as the water pressure increased with their descent, but the beast refused to release his grip on the giant sawfish until he was sure that the mutant was dead. The yeti continued to use his teeth to tear into the sawfish until the sea monster finally stopped struggling. With his ears ready to burst from pressure and his mind close to blacking out from lack of oxygen, the yeti released the dead sawfish and he began swimming toward the surface. The yeti's lungs felt as if they would explode out of his chest if they did not receive fresh air soon, and he could feel himself losing consciousness. The yeti's strokes toward the surface were slowing down as his body started to shut down. The monster started to sink back toward the ocean floor when an image of his deceased family and Armorsaur flashed into his mind. When he saw the creature who was the target of his hatred, a wave of fresh energy surged through the yeti. The beast forced his mind and body to adhere to his will, and once again, he began swimming toward the surface. Every cell in the yeti's body was screaming for oxygen when he finally saw light above him, indicating he was near the surface.

With several more powerful strokes, the yeti finally reached the surface of the water where he exhaled the air trapped within his lungs and filled them with fresh oxygen. The yeti took several more measured breaths in an attempt slow his heart rate and regain full control of his body. After floating on the water for several minutes, the yeti had managed to recover from his battle with the sawfish. The yeti roared, indicating that he had vanquished his foe then he continued his quest to find Armorsaur.

CHAPTER 8

THE SKIES OVER PERU

Chris was piloting Steel Samurai 2.0 as he and Kate flew over South America and headed for the campsite in Peru. He was concerned about how they would be received when they entered the campsite. He turned to his wife. "So what's the plan? Am I just going to land Steel Samurai 2.0 outside of the camp and then walk it in there and say that we want to be friends?"

Kate was not in the mood for Chris's sarcasm. She rolled her eyes then glared at him. "Just fly in a circular pattern around the camp. We know that they are using a ham radio system to communicate. Give me a few minutes to listen to what's going on down there. After we gauge their current situation, we will figure out the best way to approach them."

Chris gave his wife a quizzical look. "They are speaking Spanish. How are you going to know what they are saying?"

Kate shrugged. "I grew up in the southwest United States, knowing how to speak fluent Spanish there was pretty much a necessity."

Chris nodded. "As always, you continue to surprise me."

Kate smiled at her husband. "I still have a few more surprises for you if we survive this mission, flyboy. Now be quiet so I can hear what's going on."

Chris smiled from ear to ear as he looked at his wife and set a holding pattern for the mech. "Yes, ma'am."

Southern tip of Chile Pacific Ocean
Vicente Suarez had led his team to the most southern point of South American in hopes of finding a coast that was untouched by Liopleviathan and uninhabited by other kaiju. His group had been traveling for weeks and at every shoreline they checked, the team found evidence of the gargantuan kaiju coming ashore.

The team was also unable to find a safe haven for a new campsite farther inland. The inner parts of Chile were the domain of the monstrous Dipatosaurus. As large as the monster was, even he made sure to give Liopleviathan a wide berth by avoiding going to close to the ocean. The team had sighted Dipatosaurus several times as well as several other large mutants. They managed to avoid these creatures by staying to a narrow strip of land they called the neutral zone. It was a thin stretch of land roughly a mile wide that was a little over five miles from the shoreline. It seemed to represent the farthest point inland that Liopleviathan could reach and also conversely the closest point that Dipatosaurus would venture toward the area where the massive sea beast would come to land. There were a few large mutants that wandered into the neutral zone, but for the most part, the group had managed to avoid them. Vincente had decided that the team would continue to push south. He hoped they would be able to locate a stretch of land where the water was too cold for Liopleviathan to inhabit but was still close enough to the ocean that Dipatosaurus would fear encountering the sea beast and avoid the area. If Vincente's team could locate such an area, it would be an ideal place to relocate the camp to. Vincente knew that if such a place existed that it would be here at the southernmost tip of the continent.

He had not found anything on the southern coast of Chile that indicated that either Liopleviathan or Dipatosaurus had recently made landfall in the area. He was reasonably certain that Liopleviathan had not made his way this far south. Vincente was starting to think that he had found a place his people could relocate to when two dead sperm whales washed up on shore. The whales had obviously been cut in half and eaten. Even if the creature who slew the whales was not Liopleviathan, the dead mammals were a sure sign that another kaiju was in the area. If there was an aquatic kaiju lurking in the waters off Chile, it would all but destroy any chance that his people had of relocating here. The main reason that they were looking to relocate was in hopes of finding an area where their ability to fish and hunt whales would not be threatened by the presence of a giant monster.

Vincente ordered his team to stay in the area for a few days to see if the dead whales were the work of a kaiju that was passing by or of a creature that had claimed these waters as his own. On the second day of his extended watch, several of his men began shouting which roused Vincente from his sleep. He ran to the shoreline to see two sperm whales engaged in a battle with two huge tentacles. For a brief moment, Vincente began to hope that there was a small chance that his people could move here. If the tentacles belonged to a mutated giant squid, there was a chance that the beast would move with its prey. If they belonged to a giant octopus, it would move around less than a squid would but still there was hope.

Vincente's hopes were crushed when he witnessed what occurred next. One of the sperm whales was gnawing through the tentacle that was wrapped around him when a huge pincer claw reached out of the water and cut the whale in half. The second whale soon met a similar fate. A gargantuan lobster-like creature extended its legs and rose out of the water. Vicente could now see the entire body of the creature resting above the waterline. He surmised that the monster must have had its body pressed against the ocean floor as it waited to ambush the whales.

The tentacles that the beast was using to ensnare the whales writhed on the creature's face like the snakes of myth atop of medusa's head. When he saw the huge crustacean, Vincente knew that his people would never be able to relocate here. If the monster was anything like his un-mutated brethren, then it was likely he would stay in a relatively small area close to shore. Vincente was almost sure that the lobster monster's domain would end at roughly the same spot that Liopleviathan's territory started.

Vincente called for his assistant Pablo to bring over the portable ham radio that they had put together. The young man ran quickly over to his mentor and handed him the device. Vincente adjusted the setting on the radio and called back the campsite in Peru. He was still watching the lobster monster devour the remains of the whale as he made his report, "This is Vincente, we have reached the southern tip of Chile. We have found the boundaries of both Liopleviathan's and Dipatosaurus's territories, but there is another kaiju living off the coast here. It's some form of mutated giant lobster. I do not believe that we will be…" Vincente cut his report short when he saw a large swell of water approaching the lobster from behind. He watched in disbelief as the water swell slowed down to reveal the form of a gigantic white ape-like creature heading toward the lobster.

The yeti was in knee-deep water when it roared at the lobster, forcing it to drop its meal and to turn and face him. The lobster threw up its claws in front of itself as its tentacles shot out from its face and wrapped around the yeti's legs. Thousands of hooks the size of cruise ship anchors dug into the yeti's flesh. The yeti roared in pain as the lobster started to pull the primate toward him. The yeti reached down and grabbed the tentacles, and the moment that his hands grasped the slimy appendages, he unleashed his freezing touch on them. The lobster monster tried to pull his hands away from the yeti's leg, but as soon as it began to pull them away, the already-frozen solid tentacles shattered to pieces.

The yeti stepped forward and delivered a hammer strike to the center of the lobster's face that sent the monster's entire body crashing back beneath the waves. In a demonstration of incredible strength, the yeti reached down, grabbed the lobster, and lifted it over his head. The yeti roared, and then he threw the lobster onto the beach.

Ruiz had been listening to Vincente's radio transmission and he called out to his friend, "Vincente, what has happened? Are you okay?"

Vincente reported back over the radio, "A kaiju yeti! A Yetaiju has just walked out of the ocean and attacked the lobster monster! I am not sure which kaiju's territory this is and which monster is the invader."

Vincente watched as Yetaiju walked ashore and headed directly for the lobster monster. The lobster scuttled forward and grabbed Yetaiju's shins with his pincers. Yetaiju responded by delivering several more hammer fists to the lobster's head which drove it into the ground and forced the beast to release his grip on the primate. Yetaiju reached down with both of his hands and grabbed the lobster's right pincer. With one yank, Yetaiju ripped the pincer out of its socket. Yetaiju quickly repeated the maneuver on the lobster's left pincer. The disabled lobster started to scuttle toward the ocean when Yetaiju drove his right claw through the back of the crustacean's shell. Yetaiju pulled out a chunk of meat and ate it. The lobster was still trying to make its way back to the ocean when Yetaiju roared and then jumped on the fleeing monster. Yetaiju tore and pounded at the beast until it was nothing but a mix of mashed shell and meat. When the lobster was completely destroyed, Yetaiju let loose a victory roar before crouching down and devouring his kill.

Vicente had moved behind several large rocks to conceal himself from the direct sight of the kaiju. His team had gathered around him as they watched Yetaiju clash with the lobster. Vicente took a deep breath, and then he began reporting what he had witnessed, "Yetaiju has defeated the lobster kaiju, and he is currently feeding off of its remains. I can only assume that this territory now belongs to him."

Vincente had just finished his sentence when Yetaiju began sniffing the air. An odd look appeared on the kaiju's face. The monster smelled something similar to himself and yet slightly different. Equal to the primate's desire to destroy the killer of his last family was his desire to find a surrogate family to replace the one he had lost. Intrigued by these creatures who smelled like his family and yet were different, Yetaiju left his half-eaten meal and began walking toward the scent.

Vincente continued to report on what he was seeing, "Yetaiju seems to be walking in our direction. I think that he knows we are nearby."

Chris and Kate had been listening to the conversation through the radio system in Steel Samurai 2.0. As Kate was listening to the conversation, the story that her great aunt Dana had told her years ago crept back into her mind. Her aunt told her a story of hidden valley in Antarctica where she and team of friends or hers had discovered not only prehistoric beasts but also a yeti. The yeti was known to leave the valley and to abduct women from a local village. When the yeti attacked Dana's camp, her aunt's friend, Gina, gave herself up to the yeti to spare her team. The yeti took Gina back into the valley. Gina named the yeti Yukon, and she described the beast as a twenty-five-foot juggernaut. Yukon slew all manner of prehistoric beasts that they came across. Gina had also discovered that the reason Yukon was taking people was because he was a displaced alpha male who was trying to rebuild his lost family.

Kate's mind was ablaze with thoughts of what would have happened if a kaiju had settled in the valley. The beast would no doubt have decimated the animal population there while at the same time mutating some of the surviving creatures into kaiju themselves. If this creature was indeed a mutated yeti like the one her aunt had encountered, then the kaiju version of the creature could very well be the most physically powerful monster on the planet. She also realized that if Yetaiju had left the valley, then he may be looking to rebuild his family just as Yukon had tried to do decades ago. She was trying to determine the best way to announce her presence to the people of Peru, but as Yetaiju was bearing down on the team in Chile, she was left with no choice. She grabbed the radio and screamed into it in Spanish, "Get out of there! Cover yourself in something that will hide your scent!"

Surprised by the new voice on the radio, Vincente was about to ask who it was when he saw Yetaiju reaching down for him. He yelled over the radio, "It's too late he sees us! He has grabbed us and is… AHHHH!" Vincente's transmission was cut short as Yetaiju picked up all but one member of his team to examine them. Vincente dropped the radio as the one man who escaped ran off toward the ocean. Heeding the words of the woman's voice that he heard, he covered his body in wet sand.

The confused yeti was examining the humans in his hand and he briefly became aggravated that the creatures in his palm were not yetis. In his brief moment of anger, Yetaiju unintentionally froze the entire team to death. The frustrated yeti tossed the icy corpses to the ground, and then he sniffed the air again. Once he had reacquired Armorsaur's scent, Yetaiju began heading north.

Ruiz called out over the radio, "Vincente, Vincente, come in! Are you there?"

Kate spoke softly into the radio, "I am sorry, but I believe that your friend is dead."

Ruiz replied, "Who is this? Where are you from? How do you have knowledge of this Yetaiju monster?"

Kate looked at Chris. "You are speaking with Kate and Chris Myers. We are piloting a giant mech that is flying above you. We come from a settlement in North America. We come in peace. If you will give us permission to land safely, we have a good deal to discuss including ways in which we can help you!"

Ruiz thought about the request for a moment. He considered the implications of what he had just learned and how the leaders of the camp would react to it. He was about to answer when a young boy came running over to him, "Two giant beetles are coming from the forest toward the camp; we are going to need Revenant to fight them off!" Ruiz grabbed the receiver. "If what you say is true. If you have a mech, and you are willing to help us, this is your chance. Our kaiju-hybrid Revenant will soon be defending the camp against a threat from two giant insects. You can prove to the people and the leaders of the camp that you are here for our benefit if you will use your mech to help protect us from this threat."

Kate quickly responded, "We will assist you in dealing with this threat. Please send us the location of the oncoming kaiju." Ruiz quickly sent the location of the approaching beetles to Kate.

When Ruiz ended his transmission, Chris looked at Kate. "I was going to ask you what you know about this Yetaiju, but I guess that's going to have to wait, isn't it?"

Kate gave Chris a grave look. "If this giant yeti is what I think he is, then he may pose even a greater threat to us than Atomic Rex." Kate was silent for a moment as her entire body shivered. Chris had only seen his wife shake like that when she thought about one thing. He wouldn't say the name but she did. "He could pose a similar threat to Ogre if the stories my Great Aunt Dana told me are true."

The man who had covered himself in mud ran over the radio. "Hello, this is Pablo Garcia. The rest of the team is dead! The kaiju seems to have picked them up and frozen them solid. I survived by covering myself in mud. What should I do now?"

Kate quickly replied, "Track the yeti, but make sure that you continue to cover your scent; if he smells you, he will go directly for you!"

Pablo's voice was shaking with fear as he replied, "Alright, I understand. I will keep you informed of the yeti's movements."

Chris put his hand on his wife's shoulder. She squeezed it, and then she pushed the trauma of her past out of her mind by focusing on the present threat. "We can talk about Yetaiju later. Right now, we need to focus on taking out those two beetles." Chris nodded and sent Steel Samurai 2.0 flying in the direction of the attacking beetles.

CHAPTER 9

SOUTHERN NEW MEXICO

Erica Stokes and Fred Byers were sitting in a small truck and monitoring the movements of Ramrod as he roamed across the desert searching for food. The job was a relatively simple mission as the giant big-horned sheep was mostly a benign creature. They were joking around with each other and keeping an eye on Ramrod when a deafening roar emanating from the mountains echoed across the sky. The roar caused Ramrod to bolt in northwestern direction. It also caused both Erica's and Fred's hearts to skip a beat. Erica grabbed her binoculars and looked in the direction of the mountains. Her body went stiff with fear at the sight she beheld. There making his way down the side of the mountain was Atomic Rex. The most powerful kaiju in North America had crossed the Rocky Mountains and would soon be within a few days striking distance of the campsite.

Erica looked toward Fred. "Atomic Rex has crossed the mountains. Use the radio to contact the campsite and make Emily Myers aware of the situation immediately." She looked back through her binoculars at the quickly moving kaiju. Then she yelled at Fred, "Do it quickly! At the speed that Atomic Rex is moving, he will be on our location in less than thirty minutes!"

Fred grabbed the truck's radio and called back to camp, "This is Fred Smith at Station 6C! This message is for Emily Myers! We have a visual on Atomic Rex! He has crossed the Rocky Mountains and he is making his way into New Mexico! He will be at our current position within half an hour!"

Back in Washington State, Emily cursed herself for not being there with the people under her command. She closed her eyes and reminded herself that she was at camp because it was where she could most help out people by deciding how to best address a dire situation such as this. She grabbed the receiver. "Copy that!" She looked at a map of the area. "How far is your current position from the Rio Grande?"

Fred came back quickly, "We are roughly fifty miles from the closest point of the river to us!"

Emily grabbed the chart that she used to rotate the duties of people under her command. She smiled when she saw that Erica and Fred were only on the first day of their observation rotation in the New Mexico. She grabbed the receiver, "Listen to me! The two of you are going to do exactly what I say, and by following my directions, you can divert Atomic Rex away from the camp and maybe end the threat he poses forever. First, do you still have most of your food stores?

Fred took a quick inventory of their food. "Affirmative!"

Emily smiled. "Good! Get in your truck and quickly break up any meat and dried fish that you have into five equal portions. I want you to drop the first portion at your current position. Place the remaining portions on the back of the truck and make sure that they are out in the open and giving off a scent. Once you are sure the food is giving off a scent, start driving south toward the Rio Grande. As you drive, I want to drop one portion of food at every ten-mile interval."

She gave the last part of her orders in a very measured tone. "You need to drive fast enough to stay ahead of Atomic Rex, but not so fast that he can't track you. Behemoth will attack anything that comes within a five-mile radius of the river. I want you to drop the last portion of food as close to the river as you can. If you see Behemoth, turn the truck around and drive in a northwest direction at top speed. Once you feel that you are at the farthest point from which you can observe the kaiju, watch the battle and report back to me with the results."

Fred's voice came back meekly over the radio. "Ma'am, you want us to lure Atomic Rex into a battle with Behemoth."

Emily tried to speak with as much confidence in her voice as she could. "Yes. It's a variation on a plan that my father used years ago to get kaiju to kill each other. If you are successful in your mission, the best-case scenario is that the two monsters kill each other. If Atomic Rex lives, at least we will have detoured him before he wanders into our campsite looking for our food supplies.

If the Behemoth wins, then we have eliminated the threat posed by Atomic Rex. I know that I am asking a lot of you two, but I also know that you can do this."

Fred and Erica both replied with, "Yes, ma'am!" They then quickly divided up their supplies and dropped the first portion on the ground as Atomic Rex continued to make his way down the mountain.

As the kaiju made his way down the mountain, he could smell the scent of fish and meat. Saliva dripped out of the kaiju's mouth as he approached the source of the scent. When his feet touched down on level ground, the nuclear theropod ran across the scoring desert sand as if he were chasing a fleet-footed prey animal. When the kaiju reached the small pile of food, he quickly licked it up with a single swipe of his tongue. Atomic Rex then sniffed the air and caught the scent of the truck that was already seven miles down the road ahead of it. The monster roared at the fleeing vehicle, and then he took off in pursuit of it.

Erica and Fred continued to follow Emily's plan even though they were scared out of their wits at what they were doing. With each passing second, they could see Atomic Rex in the distance growing ever closer with every step. Their food drops didn't slow the monster at all. The kaiju was able to eat the small amount of food they had dropped without breaking his stride. Their truck was roughly a mile ahead of Atomic Rex when they could see the Rio Grande. When the river came into sight, they looked back to see the nuclear theropod stop dead in his tracks. They watched as Atomic Rex sniffed the air and stared at the river. The kaiju roared at the river, and then he began sprinting towards it.

Erica looked over at Fred. "I think that he smells Behemoth." Before Fred could reply, a loud grunting sound came from the Rio Grande. They watched as a mountain with a waterfall cascading down its sides rose out of the middle of the river. The gigantic hippopotamus known as Behemoth opened his jaws to show his tusks with the corpses of deer, sheep, and bison that had ventured too close to river impaled on them. When Behemoth shook his head, Erica and Fred could see the impaled corpses swinging from side to around the tusks that had become their final resting place.

Erica screamed then she turned the truck hard to the right and sped away from the creature as quickly as she could.

Behemoth stepped out of the water where he began stamping and pawing at the ground while showing his tusks and open mouth to Atomic Rex in a display that claimed the river as his territory. When Atomic Rex saw the colossal pachyderm, the thought of devouring the bulbous creature dominated the kaiju's thoughts. Atomic Rex walked toward Behemoth, and he roared at the mutant creature.

Atomic Rex took two steps to his right so that he was not directly in front of Behemoth's protruding tusks then he charged the beast. Atomic Rex wrapped his arms around the neck of Behemoth as he bit into the hippopotamus's shoulder. Behemoth barely noticed the superficial wound as his jaws snapped shut several times in attempts to crush Atomic Rex's spine. When Behemoth realized that Atomic Rex was out of the range of his jaws, the colossal pachyderm began to push his body into his adversary. While Atomic Rex and Behemoth were roughly the same height and length, the hippopotamus was by far the heavier of the two monsters.

Behemoth forced Atomic Rex to move backwards and to lose his footing, causing the kaiju to fall onto his side. Behemoth opened his mouth to drive his tusks into the kaiju, but before he could lower his head, Atomic Rex had managed to lock his jaws onto the mutant's left front leg. Atomic Rex tore a large chunk of flesh away from the leg, and then he leapt out of the way of Behemoth's head as the hippopotamus swung it at him. Atomic Rex realized that Behemoth was heavier than he was, but he also knew that he was far quicker than his plodding adversary.

Atomic Rex moved to the side of Behemoth where he reached out with his sharp claws and gouged the pachyderm from its spine to the base of its stomach. Behemoth turned toward Atomic Rex, but as he turned, the saurian monster turned with him. Behemoth's mouth snapped shut over empty air as Atomic Rex tore a large piece of flesh off the hippopotamus's rear left leg. Nearly the entire left side of Behemoth was covered in blood as Atomic Rex leapt onto the creature's back. The nuclear theropod dug his claws into the sides of the mutant, and then he reached down and bit off a mouthful of flesh from behind Behemoth's head. The giant hippopotamus shook his body and threw Atomic Rex off his back. The saurian kaiju landed on his feet on the right side of his prey. Atomic Rex slashed his claws across the right side of Behemoth, and then he bit another mouthful of flesh off the pachyderm's rear right leg.

Behemoth was swaying from side to side as blood gushed out of his body from multiple injuries. Atomic Rex could see that his adversary was quickly weakening from blood loss. The kaiju roared at the mutant, goading Behemoth into attacking him again. Behemoth opened his mouth and charged at Atomic Rex, but once again, the reptilian horror was able to side step the attack. When Behemoth's charge stopped, Atomic Rex again leapt onto the hippopotamus's back where he used his teeth and claws to tear open new wounds and increase the amount of blood that the mutant was losing. Behemoth bucked wildly, and he managed to shake Atomic Rex off his back one final time. Atomic Rex landed on his feet. He roared at Behemoth, and then he slowly started to circle his prey. The saurian kaiju watched Behemoth as the beast swayed back and forth in a feeble to attempt to maintain his balance.

Atomic Rex could see that his prey had lost too much blood to continue the battle. The kaiju roared at Behemoth before walking to the side of the creature, placing his claws on the hippopotamus's blood-covered stomach, and then pushing the beast to the ground. Atomic Rex roared loudly proclaiming his victory, and then he took a bite out of the still breathing Behemoth. The mutant pachyderm felt Atomic Rex tear five more bites of flesh off out of his body before he finally expired.

Erica was watching Atomic Rex devour Behemoth through her binoculars when the sight became too gruesome for her endure. She handed the binoculars to Fred who gasped when he looked through them. Erica picked up the truck's radio and she contacted Emily back at base, "Ms. Myers, the battle is over, and Atomic Rex is feeding off the remains of Behemoth."

Emily replied, "It will take a couple of days for Atomic Rex to eat Behemoth. You two have done well. You have brought us a precious couple of days until we have to deal with Atomic Rex again. Now hurry back home. My brother is initiating plans to evacuate the settlement."

CHAPTER 10

He breathed in the stench of death and decay as if it was the most pleasant aroma that he had ever smelled. Three kaiju lay dead at his feet and the bodies of hundreds of thousands of people littered the landscape all the way to the horizon. Revenant was in his glory as he stared at the carnage around him. In the distance, he could see another kaiju walking toward him. The beast looked like something that was half-woman and half-reptile. On the top of her head, dozens of snakes slithered and writhed over top of one another. Whatever this creature was, Revenant was determined to kill her for the offense of entering his territory. Revenant grabbed his weapons and started walking to this newest threat to his domain.

Ruiz was running up to the sleeping form of Revenant when he saw the kaiju-man's arm swing through the air and crush several trees. Revenant then lifted his hand up into the air and brought it crashing down, causing the earth beneath Ruiz's feet to shake. The terrified scientist called out to his creation, "Revenant, wake up! We need you! There are several large mutant beetles heading toward our camp."

Revenant's eyes snapped open, and his head whipped around in the direction of his creator and friend. The images from his nightmare were still fresh in his mind, and for a brief second, the thought of seeing Ruiz dead at his feet was all that the kaiju-man could focus on. Revenant stood and started walking toward Ruiz with an animalistic look on his face and his hand lifted in the air ready to strike.

Terrified, Ruiz fell to the ground and screamed, "Revenant, it's me your friend, Ruiz!" The giant continued walking toward the fallen man, and when he reached his creator, the monster roared. Revenant's fist was on its way to crush Ruiz when the human side of the kaiju-man's brain was finally to reassert itself. He forced his blow to land to the side of Ruiz, crushing a massive hole into the ground next to the man.

Ruiz was crying as he looked up at the monster who had once been a man and he spoke to it very softly, "Revenant, it's me Ruiz. I think that you were having a nightmare that carried over when you woke up, but you are good now, right?"

The kaiju-man shook his head affirmatively.

Ruiz wiped the tears from his eyes and tried to stop his heart from beating out of his chest. "Good. That's good." He took several deep breaths before speaking again, "There are two giant beetles heading toward our campsite from the east. You need to go and fight them off, but you will not be alone. We have made contact with another group of humans. They have a giant mech that will assist you in the battle. Do you understand?"

Once more, the giant nodded. He then picked up his weapons and quietly strode off in the direction of the oncoming monsters.

Chris could see two large black forms moving through the jungle. He zoomed in the mech's view to see a long black shell with a secondary shell covering the beetles' heads with a long horn-like protrusion sticking out of it. When he was a kid, Chris remembered seeing some sort of nature documentary on the rhino beetle. He had no idea if the bugs that he was looking at used to be rhino beetles. He also had no idea if that particular species of beetle lived in the Peru. All that he knew as that the mutant bugs below him looked like how he thought rhino beetles would look like. He also thought that with the mission ahead of him, the bugs were not worth wasting ammunition on. Chris had Steel Samurai 2.0 draw his sword. Then he had the mech dive straight for the giant beetles.

Steel Samurai 2.0 landed in front of the two beetles, and Chris had the mech strike the insect to its right over its shielded head with its sword. To Chris's surprise, the mech's sword bounced off the shield-like covering, and before Chris could make another move, the beetle threw itself on top of Steel Samurai 2.0 and caused the mech to fall flat on its back.

Chris and Kate were both bounced around in their seats from the impact. Kate looked over at her husband. "A beetle that size is likely to have a shell that is nearly invulnerable! We may have to knock the mutants onto their backs in order to hurt them." The cockpit of Steel Samurai 2.0 was rocked from side to side as the beetle continued to strike at the mech's head with its horn. Chris was trying to position the mech's hands under the beetle when through his outside video feed he saw the grotesque form of Revenant slam into the giant bug and knock it off Steel Samurai 2.0. Revenant roared, and then he began using his axe, knife, and foot talon to hack at the insects. Despite the fact that his weapons seemed to be having little to no effect on the beetles, the kaiju-man continued to slash at his adversaries.

Chris shifted Steel Samurai 2.0 to a standing position as he watched the video feed of the two beetles goring Revenant with their horns and forcing the monster backwards. Chris looked over at Kate. "This thing is supposed to be a soldier who died and was brought back to life then transformed into that thing by fusing his body with kaiju DNA, right?" Chris shook his head. "I thought that our reports said that the soldier was in control of that things body?"

Kate nodded. "That's what the transmissions we picked up indicated. That Revenant had the body of kaiju but the mind of a soldier.'

Chris shook his head. "I have seen plenty of soldiers fight, and I have certainly seen kaiju fighting up close." He gestured toward the screen where Revenant was now trying to the bite the beetles that were forcing him to the ground. "Whatever that thing is, it has more kaiju in its mind that it does human."

Kate sighed. "He is the only protection that the people of this campsite have, and right now, he needs our help."

Chris nodded. "Okay. You say that we need to get these things on their backs?" He looked again at the battle taking place before him with Revenant now completely on his back with both beetles on top of him. Chris shrugged. "Well, at least he makes good bait." Chris ignited Steel Samurai 2.0's foot thrusters so that the mech hovered off the ground. He then shifted the robot into a vertical position and flew straight for the two beetles. When the mech reached the giant insects, it grabbed both of them by their horns. Steel Samurai 2.0 maintained its grip when it landed between the two creatures, forcing them onto their backs.

The two giant insects' legs were flailing helplessly in the air as the beetles tried to right themselves. Chris used Steel Samurai

2.0's sword to quickly gut one of the giant insects. He then turned the mech around to see Revenant hacking away at the other downed beetle. Chunks of shell, legs, and ichor flew through the jungle as Revenant tore into the long dead mutant. The giant insect was little more than a pile of shell and goo as Revenant continued to tear into it.

Chris was unsure of what to do when he saw a man come running out of the jungle.

Ruiz looked on at Revenant in horror. He knew what was happening to his creation. What was left of the soldier's mind was slowly slipping away and the kaiju was taking over. With the American's and their mech here now, Ruiz needed Revenant to hold on to his humanity for just a little bit longer. He called to his creation, "Revenant, stop! It's dead." Ruiz looked on as Revenant continued to tear at remains of the beetle. He called again, "Revenant, it's me, Ruiz! You have won, please stop!"

Revenant's head turned toward Ruiz as the kaiju-man roared. He shook his head several times and then his body seemed to relax. The giant calmly picked up his weapons and he began heading back toward the campsite. Ruiz wiped the sweat from his brow, and then he gestured to the pilots inside of the mech to follow him back to camp.

Twenty minutes later, Chris and Kate were meeting with Ruiz and Mendoza, who for Chris's benefit, were speaking English. Kate thanked both Ruiz and Mendoza for agreeing to speak to her and Chris. After the introductions were complete, Kate started to explain her plan to the Peruvians. "Gentlemen, we had come here with a plan that would have benefited our camp and hopefully yours as well. Our original plan was to draw Atomic Rex through Central America then through the northern part of South America and into Brazil. We believe that with the kaiju who are located south of Brazil that they would create enough giant mutants to function as a sustainable food supply for themselves and Atomic Rex.

"If Atomic Rex is able to slay the kaiju in the northern part of the continent as well as Central America, we would offer to help your group relocate to an area of your choosing in Central America away from the kaiju." Kate let loose a sigh. "I fear though that a new variable has been added that must be addressed. The giant yeti, Yetaiju, as your team called him. I do not think he will act in the same manner as other kaiju." Images of her great aunt and Ogre flooded her mind. She grabbed Chris's hand to help draw strength from her husband. She looked in Chris's direction as she voiced her concerns, "For the most part, the kaiju stay in their own territory unless provoked to move into another monster's domain. If Yetaiju is what I suspect he is, then he will actively seek out humans. Decades ago, my Great Aunt Dana was part of a team that entered into an unexplored valley in Antarctica. They discovered not only prehistoric beasts there, but also a polar yeti. The story was unbelievable at the time, but in light of the kaiju that came off the island and ended civilization as we knew it, I guess I should have reconsidered that her story could have been true."

She squeezed Chris's hand even harder as she continued, "The yeti they encountered was only about twenty-five feet tall, but it was the most powerful thing they had ever seen. If a kaiju entered the valley and exposed a yeti to radiation, causing him to grow to the size he is now, the beast could rival Atomic Rex as the most powerful monster on land."

Kate squeezed Chris hand slightly harder. "There is another pivotal aspect to this story. The yeti they encountered would also take people back to its lair. My great aunt's friend was taken by the yeti, but she managed to escape the monster. She came to believe that the yeti who took her was a displaced alpha male who was looking to create a new family for himself and humans were the closest thing to his own kind that he could find. From the way Yetaiju chased your men and picked them up, I suspect that he is looking to create a new family as well." Kate began to tear up as the years she spent with Ogre ran through her mind. "Trust me. Those men are better off dead than they would be in the hands of a monster."

Kate tried hard to keep looking at the men she was speaking to so that they could see the fear in her face. "I have dealt with other monsters like Yetaiju. If he feels the need to rebuild a family, he will seek out humans because we are the closest thing to his own kind. Yetaiju will head for this campsite. He will overtake this camp and force the people here to live with him. If that happens, your people will be facing a slow terrifying death as the kaiju seeks to make them fit into his perception of how they should behave."

She wiped the tears from her eyes and continued, "In order to stop Yetaiju from coming here, I think that we need to consider leading Atomic Rex directly into the yeti's path. Pablo is still tracking the yeti. He can help us keep tabs on Yetaiju's location as we lead Atomic Rex to him. When they meet, the two kaiju will naturally be inclined to battle and hopefully, they will kill each other. If they do not outright kill each other, the victor of the battle will be in a weakened state. The original Steel Samurai was nearly able to kill Atomic Rex after he had battled Tortiraus. With Steel Samurai 2.0 and Revenant working together, there is a good chance that they can slay what is hopefully a severely wounded winner. Then, we can help you relocate your people to Central American and away from Liopleviathan."

Ruiz shook his head. "There are two problems with that scenario. The first is that as far as we can tell, Liopleviathan's range extends as far north as California. The second issue is that Revenant will soon be as great a threat to us as any other kaiju."

Mendoza looked at Ruiz. "What are you talking about? Revenant has protected us for years!"

Ruiz's entire face sank as he revealed the truth about his creation. "It's something that has slowly been happening for a while and that we knew could be a consequence of combining a human body with kaiju tissue. Revenant is losing the human part of his mind. He is slowly changing entirely into a kaiju. Aside from his recently overly aggressive actions toward the kaiju he has fought, he nearly killed me today before he realized who I was." He looked toward Mendoza. "Soon, he will be our own personal Frankenstein's Monster."

Chris never considered himself to be the smartest person on in the room, but when he looked at a situation as a soldier, he could see things from a unique perspective. It was the way he saw things when he first enacted his plan to draw the kaiju into each other's territory and it was the way he saw things now. Now, it was Chris who was grasping his wife's hand for support as he spoke, "What we need to do is clear. First, we need to have Atomic Rex move through the kaiju in Central America and the northern part of this content as quickly as possible. Steel Samurai 2.0 is best suited for this task. Once Atomic Rex is in South America, we will lead him east so that the people who are living here can make their way north into Central America. In the meantime, another team will follow Pablo's directions and take Revenant toward Yetaiju. Revenant can use hit-and-run tactics as long as possible while leading Yetaiju away from this location. The best bet would be to lead Yetaiju into the territories of the other southern kaiju."

Chris directly at Ruiz. "If Revenant goes full kaiju when leading him on this goose chase, then he will likely battle Yetaiju to the death and solve one of our problems. Once the campsite is clear, we can lure Atomic Rex back here to try and hold him in the Pacific until we encounter Liopleviathan. Atomic Rex will attack Liopleviathan and one of them will slay the other." Chris gritted his teeth as he found the next part of what he was going to say difficult to live with. "Steel Samurai 2.0 can even assist Atomic Rex when he engages Liopleviathan. The mech is fast enough in the water and has enough firepower that we can do some damage to Liopleviathan without getting too close to him." Chris shrugged. "From there, we just lead the winner of the Revenant Yetaiju encounter or whatever monster is left to face the winner of the Atomic Rex-Liopleviathan fight. Best-case scenario, they all die and the entire Western Hemisphere is kaiju free."

The three other members of the group were all looking at Chris. It was Mendoza who spoke first, "What of my people? What if Liopleviathan does not die? Then we are still left at the mercy of that monster!"

Chris shrugged. "Then you would be no worse off than you are now. It would also be a difficult migration, but at least your people would be able to move toward our camp without the fear of kaiju along the way."

Ruiz nodded. "The plan has some potential failings to it, but with both of our camps facing imminent death, I think that it is the probably the best course of action that we can take."

Kate kissed her husband. "And you always say that I am the smart one in the family."

Chris smiled at her. "Alright then, Kate and I will climb into Steel Samurai 2.0 and start working on drawing Atomic Rex south while you guys take Revenant south in search of Yetaiju and Pablo."

Kate pulled away from Chris. "I am not going with you Chris. I am going after Yetaiju." Before Chris could say a word, she cut him off, "Before you argue with me, you know that going after Atomic Rex and Liopleviathan is just as dangerous as going after Yetaiju." She leaned into Chris and hugged him. "One way or another, Chris, I need to know that threat of Yetaiju is gone. I can't have our kids living in a world where a monster can take them and keep them like pets. I won't have them live like I did with Ogre for all of those years. If we die fighting Atomic Rex without knowing if Yetaiju is dead, I'll die with the thought that our children could still be facing that possibility. I can't imagine that anything in Hell can be worse than dying with that thought on my mind. If I die chasing this monster, at least I will have the thought that you are still out there and that you can still save our kids from that fate. At the very least, I will die with hope instead of despair."

Chris looked into his wife's eyes, and while it pained him to be apart from her during what could very well be his last few days on Earth, he could see that this was something that she needed to do. He also knew that he loved her enough to let her do it. He hugged and kissed her as he whispered, "I love you." She smiled, as through her tears a quote from her favorite movie as child strangely seemed to fit the situation better than anything else she could think of. She simply replied, "I know."

When they let go of each other, she turned to Ruiz and Mendoza. "What kind of transportation do you have that can get us to Pablo?"

Ruiz shrugged. "We have a few trucks and one that is capable of transporting horses. We also have several horses. I suggest that we load the horses into the truck, and when we are near Yetaiju, we should ride the horses. If the yeti can track us by scent, the smell of the horses will help to mask our presence from him."

Kate nodded. "Alright then. We all have work to do so let's get moving."

CHAPTER 11

The sun was blazing hot, the humidity of the jungle was crushing, and the mosquitos were unrelenting. For the past two days, Pablo had been following Yetaiju as the monster made his way north and east. The young man was doing his best to track the direction and distance in which he had traveled, and every hour, he used his radio to update Ruiz and his team on his current location. Pablo was nearly exhausted. He had been moving at a quick jog for nearly two days with only a few hours rest at irregular intervals. Even when Yetaiju was walking, he was moving at a speed that Pablo was barely able to keep up with. To some extent, Pablo was pleased with this, as even when moving at a quick jog, he could only occasionally see Yetaiju in the far distance ahead of him. Most of the time, Pablo simply followed the wide path of crushed trees or huge footprints that Yetaiju left in his wake.

Pablo came across another small stream, and once again, he covered himself in mud. He was sure that Yetaiju had entered Argentina and that they were deep into Dipatosaurus's territory. Pablo was terrified at the thought of what was ahead of him. The mud that he was covering himself with seemed to be masking his scent enough that Yetaiju didn't notice him, but he had no idea if the mud would prevent Dipatosaurus or the countless giant mutants that lived in the area from noticing him. There was also they very real possibility that the mud he was covering himself with was radioactive and that he was slowing killing himself each time he applied it to his skin.

The only good thing the Pablo seemed to have going for him was that the Yetaiju was not heading directly for Peru and the campsite. The monster's northeastern track was taking him further into Argentina and heading toward the Atlantic Ocean as opposed to the Pacific. Pablo didn't know much about giant monsters or about what drove them, but what he did know was tracking and hunting behaviors. Pablo had only been a small child when the world ended. For the most part, the world of the kaiju was all that he knew. When he was an adolescent, his job was to track and hunt small game. From the way that Yetaiju would stop periodically to check out the trees and the jungle floor to the way that it would continually sniff the air and make a slight change in direction, Pablo was sure that the monstrous yeti was tracking something. Pablo shook his head and said to himself, "Heaven help whatever he is looking for when he finds it."

For a brief moment, Pablo felt as if the world had shook around him. Thinking that his body was telling him that he was exhausted and likely dehydrated, the young man decided to sit down for a few minutes before he passed out. Even if he had not been a tracker, he was sure that he could follow the path of knocked down trees crushed by Yetaiju's massive feet.

Pablo was resting with his back against the trunk of a tree when the ground shook again. A tingle ran down his spine as he began to think that the sensation of the ground shaking beneath him was not due to his lack of sleep and water. A third instance of the ground shaking was followed by two twin roars that seemed to overlap each other. Pablo looked up to see two long, thick shapes blocking out the scorching sun above him. Pablo pulled the portable radio to his chest, and then threw his body to the ground and began logrolling into the thick underbrush of the jungle. He rolled until his body struck a fallen tree, and when he looked back at the spot where he was resting only a moment prior, he saw two huge plumes of flames engulf the tree that he was sitting under and everything else around it. Even though he managed to avoid being completely incinerated by the flames, the heat from the fire still caused the exposed skin on his arms, legs, and face to blister.

The fire was spreading through the jungle, but Pablo did not dare move from his current position. The two-headed horror known as Dipatosaurus let out another twin roar before continuing to follow the path of the kaiju that had invaded his territory. Burning treetops fell around Pablo as Dipatosaurus walked through the inferno that he had created. Pablo's eyes and throat were stinging as he was nearly blinded and suffocated by the smoke that wafted from the burning foliage. He stumbled around the forest fire until he was able to find a way out of the inferno.

Once he found an area of the jungle that was not burning, he ran out of the flames in the opposite direction from which Dipatosaurus was heading. When he was clear of the flames, he coughed several times to clear his lungs, and then he called into the radio, "Ruiz, come in! Ruiz, come in! Dipatosaurus is chasing Yetaiju! At the speed he is moving, I suspect that he will catch up to the yeti in roughly fifteen minutes! Do you copy? Ruiz, do you copy? Dipatosaurus is going to engage Yetaiju!"

Ruiz replied, "I copy. What is your current location?"

Pablo breathed a sigh of relief then quickly relayed the coordinates of the forthcoming battle to Ruiz. He was waiting for a reply when all that he heard come back over the radio was Ruiz shouting, "Revenant, no!"

10 miles northwest of Yetaiju's current position

Ruiz and Kate were sitting in a truck and making their way down a trail that ran along one of the many rivers in Argentina at maximum possible speed toward Pablo's last reported position. Revenant was walking behind them with his weapons at the ready in case if they were to run into Dipatosaurus or some other large and aggressive mutants. Ruiz and Kate were conversing in Spanish, and Ruiz was amazed to hear about all of the services and infrastructures that Kate and Chris were able to establish at the camp. Kate had explained that the lack of a large kaiju swimming off their shores and the capabilities of Steel Samurai 2.0 were the main reasons why her camp was capable of establishing a thriving fishing community and desalination operation. She also pointed out that Steel Samurai 2.0 was also useful for activities such as building roads and housing in addition to fighting the occasional monster.

Kate was talking when Ruiz slammed on the breaks. Revenant had stopped walking. He could see something large in the river. The kaiju-man took a few more steps toward the river until the object came into a clearer view. He grunted when he saw a huge mutated caiman floating on top of the river. The rational human part of his mind knew that he should just keep walking because the caiman currently posed no threat to his party or to his mission. Conversely, the kaiju instincts within the giant saw the huge reptile as a threat to his territory. The monster's instincts overwhelmed the rational thoughts in his mind and the kaiju-man charged at the river.

Ruiz had just received the report from Pablo and he knew that his friend was in need of help. He was going to push the truck as hard as he could in Pablo's direction when Revenant ran toward the river. Ruiz was picking up the radio to reply to Pablo when he saw Revenant sprinting toward the river, causing him to shout into the radio.

Kate looked at Ruiz. "What is he doing? That thing was just lying in the water; it made no move to attack us."

Ruiz shook his head, "It's like I said; I believe that he is losing his grip on whatever humanity he had left. He is acting more like a kaiju with each passing day."

Revenant dove into the river and grabbed the tail of the caiman as is tried to slip beneath the water. The reptile thrashed violently and was able to free itself from the giant's grip.

Kate and Ruiz jumped out of the truck. Kate was watching the scene before her as Revenant swam after the fleeing mutant. She shook her head. "Even with the other creature retreating, he is still chasing it?" Kate turned to Ruiz. "How much longer do you think we have until he has completely given in to being a kaiju?"

Ruiz shook his head. "Not long; not only do I hope that we reach Yetaiju before Revenant becomes too dangerous for us, but I hope that we reach him soon for Roberto's sake as well."

Kate shrugged. "Who is Roberto?"

Ruiz looked toward the ground, "He was the soldier that we infused with kaiju tissue to turn him into Revenant. Technically, Roberto was dead when we found him, but I wonder how much of him was still in there when we first revived him. He never learned to expressively communicate, so we don't know for sure. I always told myself that Roberto was gone and that any intelligence that we saw from Revenant was simply the effects of a partially reanimated human brain carrying out commands, but deep down, I always worried that I had trapped a man in monster's body. If there is any part of him in there that knows it is becoming a monster in action as well as appearance, I pray that he finds the peace of death soon. I can't image the horror Roberto is experiencing if he is still aware in the creature's brain and watching his body carry out the acts that it is."

Both Revenant and the giant caiman exploded out of the water. The caiman had its jaws locked onto Revenant's right arm which held his axe. As the caiman hung on his arm, the kaiju-man continued to try and use his knife to pierce the hard caprice on the crocodilian's back.

Pablo moved away from the forest fire, and then he followed cautiously in the direction of the shockwaves caused by Dipatosaurus's footfalls. After running for nearly ten minutes, he had gotten the point where he could see Dipatosaurus from behind. He made sure to stay far enough back and downwind from the kaiju so that it was less likely to detect him. From the path of destruction that was paralleling the path that Dipatosaurus was walking in, Pablo was sure that the kaiju was going after Yetaiju.

Pablo's heart skipped a beat when he saw Dipatosaurus come to a dead stop and then heard him unleash one of his double roars. Dipatosaurus's challenge was answered by the shriek-like roar of Yetaiju. Pablo cringed when he felt the ground shaking beneath his feet as the colossal yeti sprinted toward the two-headed mutant dinosaur. Pablo grabbed the radio and yelled into it, "Yetaiju has engaged Dipatosaurus! I need you to get Revenant here and to get me away from these monsters now!"

Kate and Ruiz watched as the giant caiman rolled its body into the river and pulled Revenant by his arm beneath the water as well. They could see the water churning as the kaiju-man and the giant beast continued their struggle.

Kate heard Pablo's call over the radio and she turned toward Ruiz. "We have to go now! We can't let Pablo die out there!"

Ruiz was torn as to what he should do. In a way, he felt that Revenant was a like a son to him. He had always felt that the comparison between himself and Dr. Frankenstein was an apt one since he created Revenant from the remains of a dead man. However, unlike Frankenstein, he had not abandoned his creation. He had tried to be a friend to Revenant and to give him a purpose in life. He had hoped that by staying with his creation, he could avoid its descent into a monster like Frankenstein's beast. Ruiz could see that his efforts were in vain. He could see Revenant becoming a monster before his eyes. He also wondered though if leaving Revenant now would be akin to walking away from a friend who was dying. If there was anything left of Roberto in the giant's body, Ruiz wondered if he would want someone with him as his consciousness slipped away.

Kate settled Ruiz's internal debate for him when she grabbed him by the arm and screamed, "We can't do anything to help out Revenant, but if we act now, we might be able to save Pablo's life!" She pointed at the back of the truck. "We won't be able to go much further with the truck. Let's grab the horses and head through the jungle!" She was pulling Ruiz toward the truck as he took one last look at the river and the battle raging within it. He both hoped and feared that he would see Revenant again.

When the mutant caiman realized that he could not drown Revenant, the reptile started to pull the giant back upstream towards its lair. If the creature's death roll failed, its next option was to try and trap its prey underwater where it could slowly eat it over the course of several days. With Revenant's arm still trapped in its mouth, the reptile shot through the water like a living speedboat carrying the kaiju-man nearly a mile downstream. As the giant was being pulled through the water, he continued to stab at the thick caprice on the reptile's back.

Revenant's head slammed into rocks and fallen trees along the bottom of the river, jostling his brain and causing further damage to his already fragile psyche. When the caiman reached a group of large tree roots that intertwined on the riverbed, it tried to force Revenant into it. The reptile had the most of the kaiju-man's upper body jammed into the maze of thick roots when it the made the mistake of releasing its grip on Revenant's arm. The caiman turned around to grab the giant's legs, and in doing so, the reptile exposed its underbelly to the kaiju-man. Revenant lifted his clawed leg and drove the long talon on his foot into the caiman's chest just below its jawbone. The mutant was still swimming forward as Revenant pulled his foot back, and the result was that the talon gutted the caiman from its jaw to its tail.

Blood from the mutant filled the water and surrounded Revenant. The giant breathed in the water and the blood, allowing it to fill his lungs with the death of his enemy. Revenant pulled himself free from the systems of roots that he was tangled in, and for a brief moment, he stared at the cut-open form of the dead caiman floating in the water ahead of him. Revenant swam over to the bloody corpse and grabbed the front legs of the reptile. He ripped the front legs off the corpse, causing more blood to churn in the water. By this time, thousands of piranhas and other carnivorous fish had started to feed on the carrion in the river. Revenant stood up and lifted the carcass of the dead caiman out of the water as the surface of the river below him was alive with the activity of a feeding frenzy. The piranhas took small bites out of Revenant as he stood in hip-deep water and examined his kill. The kaiju-man took one look into the eyes of the dead mutant prior to tearing its head off then dropping its remains to the scavengers that were swarming around him.

Revenant walked over to the shore, and when he exited the river, his mind began to regain a small sense of composure. He looked around, and when he saw the truck, he headed over to it. He expected to find his friend and the woman praising him for his kill, but the truck was empty. Revenant was alone and without guidance. The kaiju-man roared in a mixture of confusion and anger. The dwindling rational aspect of his mind was concentrating on finding his friend when the rage of the kaiju took control again. With the thought of finding Ruiz at the forefront of his mind, the enraged kaiju man stalked off into the jungle.

Pablo watched in awe at the speed of the colossal primate as Yetaiju moved like a white blur as he attacked Dipatosaurus. Yetaiju wrapped his arms around both of Dipatosaurus's necks, and then he squeezed them together. Despite the fact that Dipatosaurus was significantly taller and weighed more than twice as much as him, Yetaiju lifted the front legs of the saurian kaiju into the air. When he could feel that Dipatosaurus was off-balance, Yetaiju tossed the sauropod to the ground. Dipatosaurus was laying on his side as Yetaiju walked over to him. Yetaiju was towering over the fallen monster when Dipatosaurus swung his tail around and brought it smashing into the yeti's leg. The blow caused Yetaiju to fall onto his back and allowed the massive Dipatosaurus to return to a standing position.

Dipatosaurus roared at the fallen Yetaiju as he lifted his front legs into the air. When the yeti saw the bulk of the saurian beast rising in the air above him, he immediately rolled out of the way. Dipatosaurus's legs came crushing down into the earth with such force that it not only shook the earth, but it also caused a giant fissure to split into the ground that stretched out several hundred feet from the point of impact. The fissure was so large that Yetaiju's rolling body fell into it. The gargantuan yeti fell face first into the jagged stones at the bottom of the newly created ravine. When he stood up, he found that even at his full height, he was still waist deep in the fissure.

Yetaiju looked up to see the colossal form of Dipatosaurus standing above him at the edge of the ravine he had created. Both of the monster's twin heads were rearing back, and when they came forward, a wall of flames burst out of their mouths and engulfed the yeti. When the flames enveloped him, Yetaiju experienced a level of pain that he had not felt since the blood of Armorsaur had washed over him. The entire upper half of the yeti's body was being engulfed in flames and burned by temperatures rivaling the interior of a volcano. Yetaiju threw his hands up in front of his face to protect his eyes, and when he did so, his hands instinctively unleashed the freezing power within them. A cloud of ice and snow swirled out of his hands and began shielding his body from the barrage of fire, and at the same time, healing the wounds inflicted by the flames. Dipatosaurus's fiery breath began to slowly recede from Yetaiju's body as the vortex of ice and snow grew around the yeti's body and doused the flames.

Dipatosaurus stared down in confusion at the sight of his flames receding from his intended victim. Yetaiju took advantage of his opponent's confusion by digging his claws into Dipatosaurus's right front leg and using it pull himself out of the crevice. Yetaiju was on his hands and knees in front of Dipatosaurus, and before the two-headed kaiju could pull his leg away from him, the yeti bit into the saurian beast's limb and tore a mouthful of flesh and ligaments out of it.

Dipatosaurus roared in pain and anger as he pulled his leg out of Yetaiju's grip. The two-headed monster tried to lift his legs into the air to create another crevice between himself and the yeti, but his injured leg was unable to lift itself off the ground. Seeing that his enemy was wounded, Yetaiju charged at Dipatosaurus. Pablo watched as Yetaiju attacked Dipatosaurus with a rage that he had never before witnessed. Yetaiju delivered a series of brutal punches and hammer fists to Dipatosaurus's neck and body. The injured kaiju managed to stumble backward and thrust his two heads out like twin battering rams. Dipatosaurus's heads crashed into Yetaiju's chest with enough force to knock the giant yeti onto his back.

Dipatosaurus's heads reared back then once more they unleashed a wall of fire onto the yeti. When Yetaiju saw the fire coming toward him, the intelligent beast once again activated the freezing abilities within his hands. With a vortex of snow and ice swirling around his arms, Yetaiju reached up toward Dipatosaurus's flames and started to douse them. The yeti continued to walk through the flames and douse them until he reached Dipatosaurus and delivered a blow to each of his heads, cutting off the fiery attack.

Yetaiju had learned from Dipatosaurus's previous attacks what his next move would be. The yeti waited for the two-headed monster to pull his heads back, and when they were fully retracted, Yetaiju dropped to the ground. Both of Dipatosaurus's necks extended over the yeti, and when he saw the necks exposed above him, he threw his forearm at them with all of the strength in his body. Both of Dipatosaurus's necks bowed at the middle and caused the monster to momentarily choke. With his opponent stunned, the yeti once more moved with a speed and agility that belied his gargantuan size.

Yetaiju moved around to the side of Dipatosaurus, and then he climbed onto the kaiju's back. The yeti placed his legs on either side of the giant sauropod as if it was a colossal horse. When he was firmly seated on Dipatosaurus's back, Yetaiju began pounding, clawing, and biting at the base of the two-headed kaiju's right neck. Dipatosaurus roared in anguish as blood sprayed out of the base of his right neck and onto the white fur of Yetaiju.

Dipatosaurus swung its left head around in an attempt to dislodge the yeti from its back, but when Yetaiju saw the second head coming toward him, he backhanded it away from him.

Dipatosaurus's right neck was half torn away from his body when Yetaiju grabbed the bloody neck and twisted it. There was a loud crack as Dipatosaurus's left neck snapped in half. The monster's right head wailed in pain as its lifeless left head fell to the ground. The right head was still reeling in agony when Yetaiju attacked the base of its neck. Dipatosaurus tried in vain to buck and throw Yetaiju off its back as the yeti tore the base of its right neck to shreds. Yetaiju attacked the monster's right neck until a river of blood was cascading down the front of the saurian kaiju. Once more when the neck was torn in half, Yetaiju grabbed the bloody appendage and twisted, snapping Dipatosaurus's remaining neck, killing the massive kaiju.

Kate and Ruiz saw Pablo in front of them as Dipatosaurus's body came crashing to the ground. Kate addressed Pablo in Spanish, "We thought that a series of earthquakes had hit! Was all of the ground shaking from the monsters fighting?"

Pablo just nodded as he watched the blood-soaked Yetaiju place his foot on the slain Dipatosaurus. The yeti threw his arms out at his sides, and then he unleashed a roar proclaiming his victory over the two-headed monster.

The yeti's keen eyes noticed something small moving in the trees to the south of him. He thought that he saw creatures similar to the ones that he had found after leaving the ocean, but these creatures looked different from those creatures, as if their lower bodies were misshapen and did not fit their torsos. The kaiju sniffed the air, but the scent he smelled was also different from the yeti-like creatures he encountered previously. Then he saw a third creature standing behind the misshapen creatures. This creature looked similar to a yeti like the other creatures he had encountered before and accidentally froze.

Kate saw Yetaiju eyes go wide and she grabbed Pablo's hand and began pulling on it. She screamed, "Pablo, get on the horse now!" Pablo quickly climbed on the back of the horse as Kate turned the animal around and yelled to Ruiz, "Quickly, into the jungle!"

Pablo briefly turned around to see the blood-soaked Yetaiju sprinting toward them.

CHAPTER 12

Chris's mind was flooded with a mixture of emotions as he flew Steel Samurai 2.0 over Mexico and toward Atomic Rex. He had grown so used to having Kate with him that not having her in the mech next to him felt as if he was missing a part of himself. Kate was the voice of reason and the influence that helped to keep him calm and focused on his missions. She was the person who kept him from giving into emotions such as despair and anger. When they discovered that Atomic Rex was still alive, Chris blamed himself for not following him into the lake and making sure that the monster's life had ended. Chris felt as if it was his responsibility to hunt down the kaiju and put an end to the ever-looming threat that Atomic Rex posed to the human race.

Kate was the person who told him that the Atomic Rex was not his own personal white whale. She pointed out the fact that not only would they have both died if he took the damaged mech into the water after the monster, she also noted that if the mech had been destroyed that they would not have been able to use Steel Samurai 2.0 to establish their current settlement. Chris had always viewed himself as a ship out to sea and Kate as his lighthouse. He was the ship trying to battle the incomparable power of the ocean itself to help bring people ashore to safety. The problem was no matter how hard he fought against the waves, it was a pointless endeavor if he didn't know which direction land was. Kate was the lighthouse that guided him safely to home. She was the person that helped to make sure that all of his efforts were directed toward a successful outcome as opposed to being a ship in a storm that constantly struggled to stay afloat against the waves.

He looked over at Kate's seat to see that she wasn't there. He understood why she wasn't there and he supported her in her decision. He knew that she felt the need to confront this yeti, not because she felt the need to defeat it, but because she needed to know that her children would never face the same horror that she had at the hands of Ogre.

Chris started to wonder if this time it was he who needed to be Kate's lighthouse. If he should have been the one to point out to her that her white whale was a giant white yeti spawned in her memories of her time with Ogre. Chris tried to push these thoughts aside and focus on the mission at hand. He turned on his radio and smiled as he thought about talking to his children for the first time in several days.

He called out over the radio, "Emily, Kyle, come in; this is Dad in Steel Samurai 2.0."

Emily's voice came back over the radio, "Dad, it's Emily! Where is Mom?"

Chris could not only hear but feel the tension in his daughter's voice as only a father could. He tried to think of his wife and to sound as calm and reassuring as she would have. "We had a slight change in plans. She is working with a team of people from the campsite in Peru to address an issue they are facing. What's going there, and what is Atomic Rex's current position?"

Emily's quickly informed her father of everything that had happened since he had last left their campsite. "Atomic Rex crossed the Rockies near the Rio Grande. I had one of our teams lure him to the river where he engaged in a battle with Behemoth. Atomic Rex slew the giant hippo, and I thought that we had bought ourselves a couple of days, but the kaiju was ravenous after going so long with a limited food supply." She took a deep breath. "It only took Atomic Rex less than a day to devour the remains of Behemoth. After he had picked the mutant's bones clean, he started heading north. Kyle is fairly certain that he is coming here after the dried fish we have in our food stores. We relayed the information to the council and suggested that they evacuate the campsite, but they refused to do it! They still feel that it's suicide to start abandoning the campsite. Kyle tried to convince them that not preparing for an evacuation was resigning us to a death sentence, but they are not taking him seriously because he is so young. We need Mom! She's the only one who can convince them that we need to be ready to run if we have to!"

Chris closed his eyes and wished his wife was there for a moment before realizing that she was counting on him to be able to handle situations like this. He opened his eyes and spoke slowly into the radio, "Listen carefully to me, honey; first, give me Atomic Rex's current position."

Emily quickly replied, "He is in the northwest corner of New Mexico and heading in the northwestern direction."

Chris replied calmly, "Okay, I need you to..." Chris purposefully cut short his transmission, and he began sending a message via Morse code over the radio to his daughter. He suspected that the council members were listening in and perhaps even intercepting Kate's attempts to contact them. Chris did not want those power-hungry fools to hear what he was saying to Emily. He had taught Emily Morse code years ago and he hoped that she still remembered it. Through the use of the code, he told Emily the plan that he and Kate were trying to carry out. He also told her to work with her brother and other trusted people in the camp to start making preparations to evacuate the settlement in case if he was unable to change the course of Atomic Rex or if the kaiju killed him. He informed her that Kate had a radio, and they should both keep trying to reach her via Morse code. Lastly, he told his daughter that he loved her and that he was immensely proud of her before ending by questioning her if she understood everything.

Emily typed back in Morse code that she got the entire message and that she loved her father, and she was more proud of him than any daughter had ever been of her father. Then she told him to worry about the monster, because she and Kyle would take care of the campsite and her mother was more than capable of taking care of herself.

Chris smiled and tears began to form in his eyes as he was filled with pride and happiness. Kate might not have been there with him physically, but her spirit, courage, and intelligence was still with him through their children. Talking with his daughter gave Chris the sense of focus and direction that he needed. As he flew into New Mexico, he could see the kaiju on his radar. The monster was heading for his children and for his home, and there was no way in hell that he was going to let the monster reach them.

Emily turned off the radio and ran off to find Kyle. She found her brother in their family cabin. He and several of his friends were standing around a table where they were discussing the status of the food supplies. Knowing that the other people could be trusted, she quickly cut in on the conversation, "I just finished talking to Dad. He wants us to start preparing the campsite for an emergency evacuation."

Kyle looked at his sister and smiled. "Great minds think alike, I suppose. Those idiots on the council are going to get everyone in the campsite killed with their stubborn desire to prove Mom wrong at any cost." He pointed to the drawings on the table. "We are currently looking at the food supplies and the paths that we can get the most amount of food onto the ships without drawing too much attention to ourselves." Kyle looked toward his sister. "I think that I have found the route least likely to draw attention, but we are going to need to take out the guard that the council had placed around the supplies. Knocking people unconscious is not something that I am particularly well versed at, but I think that I might know someone who is more capable of doing something like that." Kyle smiled at his sister and she returned that smile while nodding her head with great enthusiasm.

Steel Samurai 2.0 was streaking over New Mexico and quickly closing in on Atomic Rex. When Chris saw the monster, he considered his options. He could use his long-range guns and missiles to fire on the kaiju. Chris knew firsthand how aggressive the monster could be, but there were several downsides to using long-range weapons. First, there was the slim chance that the monster would not be sufficiently aggravated by a long-range attack to turn away from his current course and chase the mech. There was also the fact that Chris knew that if he lived long enough, he would have to take on the massive Liopleviathan, a creature that was roughly eight times the size of Steel Samurai 2.0. Chris knew that he needed to save some of his long-range weapons not only to confront that beast, but also for the entire rest of the journey ahead of him. Lastly, there was still the fact that he hated Atomic Rex and that by having Steel Samurai 2.0 pound on the creature, it just made Chris feel better. Despite his feelings, Chris knew that if he was going to attack Atomic Rex head-on, that he needed to smart about how he did it. As Steel Samurai 2.0 was closing in on the kaiju, Chris considered the upgrades that had been made to the mech since it had last fought the nuclear theropod. With the upgrades in mind, Chris aimed the mech directly at Atomic Rex's hips.

Steel Samurai 2.0 slammed into Atomic Rex and tackled him to the ground at just under Mach 1. Chris pushed Atomic Rex through nearly a mile of rock and sand before friction brought them to a stop. Before Atomic Rex even had the chance to realize what had happened, Chris delivered two roundhouses punches to the monster's jaw, rocking its head from side to side. With Atomic Rex laying on the ground, Steel Samurai 2.0 reached down and grabbed the kaiju's tail. Chris then had Steel Samurai 2.0 accelerate in a southern direction while dragging the kaiju behind it.

The mech approached Mach 1 within seconds, creating a sonic boom that further stunned Atomic Rex. He reached Mach 2 at the thirty-second mark. He looked at the rearview video feed to see that with the amount of friction they were generating, even Atomic Rex's nearly indestructible scales were starting to be torn apart. Steel Samurai 2.0 cleared the Mach 3 mark at forty seconds and that was when he saw Atomic Rex's scales giving off a bright blue glow as the kaiju prepared to unleash his Atomic Wave attack. Chris held onto the monster's tail for another three seconds before letting go just as the mech cleared Mach 4. Steel Samurai 2.0 had no sooner released the kaiju's tail than the Atomic Wave cascaded out of the monster's body. Even at the speed that it was flying, Steel Samurai 2.0 was not able to fully outrun the blast. While Chris had managed to get the mech far enough away from ground zero to avoid taking any major damage, the shockwave still sent Steel Samurai 2.0 tumbling across the desert landscape.

When Chris was able to stop the mech from rolling, he turned around to see Atomic Rex picking himself up off the ground. Chris had seen kaiju's amazing regenerative abilities before, but he was still in awe of them as he watched the entire outer layer of Atomic Rex's scales regrow themselves within seconds. What had moments ago been exposed muscle tissue was now completely regrown scales.

Atomic Rex's eyes opened wide as he roared at the mech with an anger that he reserved for no other creature. The kaiju remembered his past battles with the robot. He remembered how the mech had nearly killed him when it drove a sword through his torso. Atomic Rex had long desired to destroy the metal giant, and now it had attacked and hurt him again. The nuclear theropod lowered his head and charged at Steel Samurai 2.0. Chris knew that the monster was able to run at speeds well over one hundred miles per hour, and now that he was sure Atomic Rex was sufficiently angered enough that he would chase him, Chris took to the sky and headed toward the Sea of Cortez.

CHAPTER 13

ARGENTINA

Kate, Pablo, and Ruiz were riding their horses through the jungle of northern Argentina at full speed and still Yetaiju was quickly closing in on them.

Pablo was holding onto Kate as she yelled out to Ruiz, "I thought that you had said the horses would mask our scent from the yeti!"

Ruiz screamed back, "I think that he saw us on the horses! It seems that we may have gravely underestimated the intelligence of the monster!"

Kate shook her head in disbelief. Pablo did not understand what Ruiz had meant with that statement. He leaned in toward Kate and asked, "What does he mean that we underestimated the yeti's intelligence?"

Kate was about to answer when a loud roar echoed through the air behind them. A moment later, they could feel the ground rumbling and hear trees being smashed to a pulp. Kate quickly explained to Pablo what Ruiz was implying, "Yetaiju is smart enough to know that we are riding on the horses and that they are masking our scent. He saw us on the horses, and now instead of trying to track our scent, he is tracking the scent of the horses!" She called out to Ruiz again, "How far are we from drawing the Yeti into Dragonus's territory!"

Ruiz took a look at the area around him and tried his best to gauge their position. He yelled back to Kate, "We are roughly twenty miles from the outskirts of Dragonus's domain, but even on flat land, that would be the maximum distance that the horses could run before exhausting themselves. Moving through the jungle like this will sap their strength even more." There was another roar and Ruiz gave Kate a worried look. "I don't think that any of that will matter soon, though! Yetaiju is going to catch up to us within the next ten minutes at the speed he is running!"

The only other option that Ruiz could currently think of was the river. He guessed that it was roughly two miles ahead of them. He yelled to Kate, "Push the horses as hard as you can, the river is a little bit ahead of us! If we can reach it, we may run into Revenant!" Ruiz was silent for a second before continuing, "Hopefully, there is still some part of the man he was once inside of the monster, and when he sees us, he will protect us!"

Kate kicked her heels into her horse, urging the animal to speed up, and when she caught up to Ruiz, she yelled, "Even if he has fully given into his kaiju instincts, he might perceive this area as his territory and attempt to attack Yetaiju for entering it!"

Ruiz simply nodded in reply as he held on to what he knew was a slim hope that Revenant still had a shred of humanity left within him.

The kaiju-man continued to stalk through the jungle. His thoughts remained fixed on finding the man and the woman that he had entered the jungle with, but his intentions toward the humans were slowly drifting into the motivations of a monster. When he had exited the river, there was a part of Revenant's mind that still had some visage of the man who was formerly Roberto, but as he walked through the jungle, the human part of his mind slowly faded into oblivion. Whatever was left of Roberto was gone forever. Revenant was no longer a kaiju-man; he was simply a kaiju. When the last bits of Roberto's thoughts were gone, Revenant looked at the axe and knife in his hands and he had no concept of what they were. The kaiju let the weapons fall to the ground as if they were meaningless to him. What had been left of Roberto had hoped to find the man one last time and to protect him as long as he could. Ironically, Roberto's last thoughts of friendship toward Ruiz had become a death sentence for his friend and creator. The kaiju section, or Revenant's mind, was focused on finding the man and the woman who he pictured in his head, but instead of protecting them, he was focused on killing them.

The monster was able to detect the scent of death ahead of him and he walked directly toward it. Revenant came across the carcass of Dipatosaurus. The kaiju was already covered in buzzards and flies that were feasting on his radioactive remains and would now likely become giant mutants themselves as a result of feeding on the dead monster.

Revenant took a quick survey of the area, and he was able to detect the scent of another monster as well another scent that was familiar to him. The familiar scent belonged to horses, and while Revenant could picture the animals in his mind, he had no idea of why he knew what a horse was. The kaiju looked in the direction that other monster had run off in. Revenant roared, and then he followed Yetaiju's path deeper into the jungle.

Yetaiju's mind was ablaze as he ran through the jungle. He was sure that he had seen yeti-like creatures. What he did not understand was how these creatures had somehow bonded their scent with that of another creature, but now that he knew that the small yeti creatures were sharing the scent of the four-legged animals, they were easy for him to track. The small creatures were the closest thing that he had seen to his own kind, and the urge to find them and to build a new family drove the former alpha yeti onward. He was desperate to catch these creatures, and with each step, he was getting closer to that goal.

Ruiz pulled his nearly exhausted horse to a stop when they reached the river. The slim hope that Revenant was still anywhere near the river quickly faded from his mind. He yelled out to his creation, but there was no return roar, nor did he see the kaiju-man walking toward him. He could feel the ground shaking as Kate and Pablo pulled their horse to a stop next to him.

Kate took a quick look around, and when she saw that Revenant was nowhere in sight, she quickly formed an alternative plan. She shouted, "Quickly, we have to get the horses across the river!"

Ruiz looked at her in surprise. "We have already seen that giant mutants live in the river! We should try run alongside it! It's our only hope!"

Kate screamed at him as she directed her horse into the water, "Yetaiju is going to be on us in a minute or two! Running alongside the river would only buy us a few more minutes before he caught us! This is the only way!"

Ruiz did not see how they stood any better of out running the yeti on the other side of the river than they did running alongside it, but not wanting to die alone, he urged his horse into the river as well. He heard Yetaiju roar again behind him, and he was terrified that he was experiencing the last few moments of his life on this planet. Ruiz was halfway across the river when he saw Kate and Pablo's horse climbing out of the water on the opposite riverbank. To his horror, he watched as Kate pushed Pablo off the horse and onto the muddy riverbank. He thought that Kate was trying to lighten the horse's load so that it could run faster, but then she jumped off the horse as well and smacked the animal in its backside, causing it to run into the jungle. She then bent down and began smearing mud on herself.

Pablo yelled at Kate, "Without the horse, we are dead! What have you done?" She yelled at him, "Remember that the mud hides our scent. So quickly cover yourself and hide your scent! He is tracking us by the horses' scents! If we can cover our scent and hide while the horses keep running, he may chase them an overlook us!"

Pablo nodded in reply and began covering himself in mud. When Ruiz reached the far side of the riverbank, he jumped off his horse, smacked its backside, and sent it running into the jungle. Kate and Pablo had moved roughly fifty feet from where they had come ashore where they were lying face down in the mud and urging Ruiz to do it with them. Ruiz pulled his body through the mud covering himself with as much of the wet sand as he could. He was roughly halfway to where Kate and Pablo were when Yetaiju's head became visible in the distance. All three people stuck their faces in the mud as the yeti approached the river.

Yetaiju stopped just short of the river where he stood and sniffed the air. He could smell the horses' scent on the other side of the river. The kaiju roared, and then he placed one massive foot in the river. The kaiju's big toe landed less than ten feet from Ruiz's body. Had the colossal digit landed on him, it would have crushed the scientist to death. Yetaiju pulled his foot out of the river and took off into the jungle after the fleeing horses.

The three humans waited several minutes before fully pulling their bodies out of the mud. Pablo was the first person to speak, "Now what do we do?"

Kate looked at the river. "We have a truck a couple of miles downstream. Let's see if we can't hike back to the truck and find a place shallow enough for us to cross." She pointed to the path of smashed trees that Yetaiju has left in his wake. "Most of the trees that the monster stepped on have been depressed below ground level by his weight. He has inadvertently created a makeshift road for us to follow. We still need to try and keep that monster away from your camp until Chris can draw Atomic Rex down here." She gestured to the radio in Pablo's hand, "Does that thing still work?"

Pablo held up the radio to show her the water pouring out it as he shook his head.

Kate shrugged. "Well, then we definitely need to find the truck because it has the only other working radio that we know of between here and your camp."

The two men nodded and they followed Kate as she began walking alongside the riverbank back toward the truck.

CHAPTER 14

Emily, Kyle, and three of their friends were hiding in the trees overlooking the food supply barracks. Kyle whispered to the group, "Okay, so here is the plan. Mike and Carmello, you guys go to the families on this list and start telling them to prepare for an evacuation." He handed the list over to his friends. "They are all people that we can trust to not make the council aware of what we are doing. Tell them to keep quiet about it but also to move quickly."

He looked toward his other friend. "Charles, you and I are going to help Emily disable Sean McDuffy; he is the man on guard duty tonight." Kyle sighed. "It's just our luck that the six foot four tower of power would be on guard duty tonight. I will charge him head on and keep him occupied as long as I can while you two sneak around behind him and knock him out with a rock or something."

Charles nodded, while Kate shook her head. "Little brother, he is twice your size. You wouldn't even be able to take one punch from that guy." As she was talking, she pulled some rope out of her pocket and tied her hair in a ponytail, "There are plenty of other ways to disable a man." She handed Kyle her radio. "Take this. My team is still tracking Ramrod's movements, but I won't be able to use it for a while." Emily then grabbed Charles's hand. "You come with me and just follow my lead."

Kyle gave his sister a confused look. "What are you going to do?"

Emily smiled. "He's been after me for a while. I plan to use the fact that he likes me to my advantage." She walked out of the woods with Charles close behind her.

Emily did her best bounce a little as she walked and to make sure that she was smiling and giggling as she approached the guard. Her father had taught her a great many things that helped her to survive in the harsh world they lived in. Emily was well versed in hand-to-hand combat, the use of long-range weapons such as arrows and rifles, and she could even pilot Steel Samurai 2.0 if she needed to. She was thankful to her father for teaching her all of those things, but it was her mother teaching her how to use her good looks to put a man off guard and acquire what she wanted from him that often times she felt were her most powerful weapons.

When Sean saw Emily bouncing toward him, he smiled and called out to her, "Hey Myers, what are you doing out here?" He looked behind her at Charles and added, "And what's that guy doing out here with you?"

She walked up close to Sean, placed her hand on his shoulder, and leaned in toward his ear as she whispered, "He is not here for me. He is here for you."

Sean jerked his head away from her, "What! I don't want anything to do with that guy."

Emily laughed. "Silly boy. He is here to take over guard duty for you so that you can do things with me." She traced his finger across his chest as she spoke, "I know that you have been after me about going for a swim for a long time. I know it seems like I turned you down a couple of times because I was busy, but it was really because my dad is so overprotective of me and he would insist on going along with us." She put her face less than an inch from Sean's face. "Right now, my dad is gone, and he won't be back until tomorrow."

Sean's heart was racing as he looked at the beautiful girl. "Look, I would really love to go for a swim with you, but it's my shift on guard duty. Even if Charles took my place, what if one of the council members comes by to check on me?"

Emily laughed again. "Charles will tell them that you got sick, saw Charles walking by, and asked him to take over for you."

Sean shrugged. "I don't know, Myers. I don't want to get those guys angry with me. Can't we do this some other time?"

Emily took a few steps away, and then she turned her back to him and took off her shirt to reveal her bare back. "If that's how you feel, but next time my dad might be there, and he will insist that I wear clothes while I am swimming, but I usually feel a little too confined when I wear my clothes in the water." She tossed her shirt to Sean and pointed to the far side of the woods from where her brother was hiding. "I am going for a swim; if you want to come join me, the ocean is that way. Just bring that shirt with you so I have something to put on when I get out of the water." Emily laughed again, and then darted off into the woods.

Sean quickly handed the keys for the food supplies to Charles, and then he took off into the woods after Emily.

Kyle came running down to the barracks. He stopped when he reached Charles who was still staring at the woods in the direction that Emily had run off in. Kyle nudged his friend with his elbow. "Come on, we have got work to do."

Charles stammered, "Your sister just took her shirt off in front of us."

Kyle sighed. "I know. Please don't remind me." He took the keys from Charles and unlocked the door to the barracks. He took a look at the food stores. Kyle pointed to their supplies of dried fish and salted meats. "We need to take about one-third of this to the fishing ships. I have already talked to the captains of the Sea Star, the Lucky Dragon, and the Orca. They think it's a good idea to be ready to evacuate with the threat of Atomic Rex in the area." He grabbed a flatbed cart from inside the storehouse and looked at Charles, "We will need to work fast. I don't know how long my sister can keep Sean busy."

Charles laughed. "I'd like to be the one keeping her busy."

Kyle sighed. "Shut up and help me start loading this cart."

The boys spent the next hour making trips to and from the ships with cargo. They used a path that ran through the woods to the ships to reduce the chances of them being seen by any of the council members. For the last fifteen minutes of their work, Mike and Carmello had returned to help them. Once they had loaded a sufficient amount of supplies onto the ship to last the members of the campsite for a little over two weeks Kyle, Mike, and Carmello went back to their hiding spot in the woods while Charles resumed his faux guard duty. Charles was standing in front of the door for roughly ten minutes when Emily and Sean came walking back from the ocean.

Emily was still bouncing and laughing while Sean was panting behind her. She stopped short of the door and waited for an obviously exhausted Sean to catch up. She quickly walked over to

Charles who was staring at how tightly her wet clothes were clinging to her body. Emily gestured for him to shift her eyes up toward her face, and then she asked him quickly, "Is everything done?" The teenager nodded in reply.

Sean was still panting as he walked up to Emily and Charles. He gestured toward Charles. "Anybody come by?"

Charles smiled. "There wasn't a soul in sight."

Sean nodded and took the keys back from him. He then looked at Emily. "Geez, Myers, you can sure as hell run and swim fast!"

She smiled leaned over and kissed him on the cheek. "That's for your efforts. If you want something more next time, you are going to have to catch me." She winked at the boy. "Start jogging and swimming every morning. I promise it will be worth your while in the end."

Sean slumped down against the wall. "I'll start first thing tomorrow morning." Emily smiled and started walking away. Sean called after her, "The next time I have guard duty is a week from today. Bring your little friend back to cover for me. I promise by then I will be in good enough shape to catch you!"

Emily ignored the guard as she and Charles walked over to woods and to her brother. When they reached the woods, Kyle handed his sister her radio. Then he sighed and gave her a disgusted look. "Really? That guy? For an hour?"

She waved her brother away. "Give me more credit than that! He chased me around the woods for twenty minutes and then another half an hour in the water. He may have some muscle, but he can't move to save his life, let alone catch me. All that he got was a glimpse to get his attention and enough teasing to keep him interested until you guys were able to raid the supplies." She smiled. "I have to admit though, he is easy on the eyes."

Kyle sighed. "Whatever, let's get out of here before someone notices us."

The group started walking back to Emily and Kyle's home when Emily's radio came to life. "Emily Myers, come in. Emily Myers, come in! This Erica and Fred; we have an emergency situation, do you copy?"

Emily grabbed her radio and yelled into it, "I hear you! What's going on?"

Erica's voice came back over the radio, "It's Ramrod. He bolted when Atomic Rex came down out of the Rockies. It took us a while, but we just found his location again. He must have run to the coast then decided to head north." There was a short pause before Erica continued with her report, "He must have been scared pretty good because he is not acting like himself. We just saw the last town that he came across. He destroyed everything in it by either ramming through it or stomping it to dust." Erica did her best to stay calm, but Emily could hear the fear in her voice. "If he stays on his current path, he will enter our campsite within four hours!"

Emily quickly replied, "Copy that. Continue to watch Ramrod and keep us informed of his location. We will attend to things here. Over and out!" She looked at her brother. "The ships are ready to go and most people are prepared for an evacuation, right?" Kyle nodded in reply. Emily began to walk faster as she talked and the boys had to start a slow jog to keep up with her. She looked at her brother. "If Dad and Steel Samurai 2.0 were here, Ramrod wouldn't be a problem, but without him, we are facing a real crisis. How long will it take to evacuate the entire camp?"

Kyle did some quick calculations in his head. "Even with the preparations that we have made four hours will be cutting it close."

Emily sighed. "Okay, then we need to start working on evacuating the town and working on slowing down that big goat!" She grabbed Mike and Carmello. "Go to the houses that you warned and tell them that we are going to need to evacuate sooner than we thought." Next, she turned to Charles. "Go and get Sean. Tell him to meet me at the weapons barracks and tell him that this time it's not for fun." Lastly, she grabbed her brother. "You come with me. We are stopping at home so you can get a pen and paper and then we are going to the council leader's place."

Ten minutes later, Emily was pounding on the door of the council leader. The half-asleep old man took his time coming to the door. He was surprised to see Emily and Kyle standing there, but before he could say a word, Emily started yelling at him, "Listen, old man, I am not as diplomatic as my mother! Ramrod is coming toward camp, and he will be here in less than four hours. My brother and I are going to try and divert him from the campsite, but in the likely event that we fail in that mission, we need to evacuate the camp." She grabbed the evacuation directions from her brother. "We have already alerted most of the people to start evacuating. The ships are in the harbor loaded with food supplies and ready to go. Take these directions; they are idiot proof, so even you should be able to follow them!"

She then grabbed the council leader by the collar of his shirt. "The lives of everyone in the camp are at stake, so it's time for you to put your cards on the table, too. Have you been blocking communications from my mother to me and the camp?"

The old man nodded as he looked away from her. "Yes, we have been intercepting your mother's communications and keeping them from you. We hoped that she might try to relay some important idea to you that we could claim as our own and use to sway the perception of the campsite into my favor."

Emily was furious at the power-hungry old man. She wanted to knock him out cold or to expose him as the fraud that he was to the people of the campsite who still looked at him as a valid leader. As much as she wanted to do those things, she knew that is not what he mother would have done. Her mother would have acted in the best interest of people in the campsite. She took a step closer to the council leader. "These people need a leader to save them and my mother isn't here. You may not be much of a leader, but you are all that they have got right now. Just follow those directions, and when you tell people something, try to sound confident. The boats will take you to a location that has already been scouted far north of here. Keep your radio on. My team and I will contact you if we are successful in diverting the monster."

She pulled the old man even closer to her so that there was only an inch of space between their eyes. "As of right now, you will stop blocking communications from my mother. We are trying to do everything that we can to save lives." She dropped her voice an octave. "I am trying to be as diplomatic as my mother would be toward you, but make no mistake, I am not her. If I find out that you have blocked any more communications in a pathetic attempt to make yourself look better at the expense of putting everyone else's lives in danger, I will kill you myself as public service, consequences be damned! Do you understand?"

The council leader nodded in reply. Emily smiled at him. "Good. Then get going; I have a defense perimeter to set up." She then turned and jogged off in the direction of the weapons barracks.

CHAPTER 15

COSTA RICA

Chris checked his location, and he was amazed that he and Atomic Rex had managed to reach the coast of Costa Rica in less than four hours. While Steel Samurai 2.0 had been flying over the water at a decent speed, the fact that the kaiju was able to match that speed while swimming was a testament to Atomic Rex's sheer strength and versatility.

Chris steered the mech toward the shoreline and landed it on the beach. He looked out to see Atomic Rex swimming above the water and looking in the sky for the mech. Chris sneered at his old nemesis. "Here I am, monster, now come and get me." He then armed two of the missiles located in Steel Samurai 2.0's chest and fired them at Atomic Rex. The water around the kaiju erupted into the air as the missiles exploded against the kaiju's nearly invulnerable scales. Atomic Rex roared in anger, and then he started swimming toward the shoreline.

Chris readied himself for the game of cat and mouse that would soon be taking place across the interior of Costa Rica. Chris took some solace in the fact that he knew he would not have to evade Atomic Rex for long because Slaughterhouse would already be looking for the nuclear theropod. The kaiju seemed to have some sixth sense that alerted them as to when another kaiju had entered their territory. All Chris had to do was to make sure that Steel Samurai 2.0 didn't take on too much damage while waiting for Slaughterhouse to show up. When Atomic Rex reached the shore, Chris had the mech lift his arm and fire a burst of rounds from the mech's high-powered machine guns. Chris could see the bright orange bullets as they streaked through the air and bounced off Atomic Rex. Chris was well aware of the fact that the bullets wouldn't hurt the monster, but they did accomplish the goal of aggravating the kaiju.

Atomic Rex roared at the hated Steel Samurai 2.0. The kaiju then lowered his head and charged at the mech only to have the annoying robot take to the sky and fly out of his range before he was able to reach it. Atomic Rex shook his head in frustration and roared a challenge at the robot that had vexed him for so many years. The kaiju was used to having other monsters accept his challenge and fight him head on, but the mech continued to attack then back away.

Chris knew exactly how much space he needed to keep between Steel Samurai 2.0 and Atomic Rex to stay clear of the kaiju's Atomic Wave attack, and he was staying a good hundred feet outside of the safe minimum distance. Chris continued to fire bullets and maintain that distance while he kept an eye on his radar. This pattern continued for roughly fifteen minutes until he picked up a large radar signal coming toward him from the south. He smiled. "Perfect. Exactly the direction that I need to lure this monster in." He changed Steel Samurai 2.0's course so that it was slowly heading south as Atomic Rex continued to chase it.

Chris led the kaiju south for another half hour as the large radar signal continued to close on their position. When the radar target was within a half a mile of his position, Chris stopped firing at Atomic Rex and he took the sky. Atomic Rex looked up at the mech and roared when a scratchy triple moo sound caught his attention. Both Atomic Rex and Chris shifted their attention to the new kaiju that had entered the fray.

Chris has seen numerous frightening kaiju over his two decades of battling monsters but none of them was as nightmarish as the abomination that was Slaughterhouse. The creature was a fused-together atrocity of three different bovine creatures that had merged into a single one hundred and thirty foot tall kaiju. The monster's body was fused together in a fashion that defied all laws of biology and life itself. Slaughterhouse had a central body that all of its other appendages protruded from. The beast had hardly any outer skin on it at all. As Chris looked at Slaughterhouse, he could see all of the exposed muscles, veins, tendons, and ligaments that held the creature together. Chris thought to himself that every step the creature took must have brought it nothing but agonizing pain.

One of the kaiju's bull-like heads sprouted out from a neck which was connected to the shoulders in the manner that any bull's head would connect to its body. This head was the only one of the three that the monster possessed that had any skin attached to it all. The monster second's head was placed directly in the middle of its back. The second skinless head faced forward and peered out over the rest of the kaiju's body like the bridge of a cruise ship. The bovine creature's third head stuck out from its lower right rear hip. Like the second head, the third head was completely devoid of any outer covering. Each of the three heads possessed thick horns that sprouted out of them.

The monstrosity had four legs underneath its body which supported its weight. Directly opposite of those legs where four more legs which protruded out of the monster's back. These four legs were kicking aimlessly at the air above the abomination. In between the front four legs of the monster were two more legs sticking out of his shoulder blades on both sides of his body.

As horrifying as the exposed muscles and extra misplaced limbs and heads were on Slaughterhouse, the most grotesque feature of the kaiju were the flies. There was an ever-present black cloud of flies that leapt on to and off of Slaughterhouse as he moved. Most of the flies were normal-sized insects, but around twenty percent of the flies that had been feeding off the exposed flesh of the kaiju for a while had mutated and grown to the size of small cars. Chris was also able to see several large patches of white moving around on Slaughterhouse which he could only assume were maggots that had been born on the seemingly undead creature and were now feeding off it.

Slaughterhouse's three heads mooed in unison as all of its hooves pawed at the ground and air signaling a challenge to Atomic Rex. The nuclear theropod responded with a roar of his own, and then the two kaiju charged each other. Just prior to reaching Atomic Rex, Slaughterhouse lowered his front head and brought it up when the two monsters collided. The move resulted in Atomic Rex being knocked back and to his left. Despite the blow, Atomic Rex had managed to maintain his footing. The reptilian kaiju was shaking his head in an attempt to recover from the collision when Slaughterhouse charged him again and drove his front horns into Atomic Rex's midsection, knocking the kaiju to the ground.

Atomic Rex had no sooner hit the ground than he swung his tail at the set of front legs that Slaughterhouse was supporting himself on. The tail knocked the legs out from under the bovine horror, but as the beast fell to its left side, the two legs sticking out of that side of its body came into contact with the ground and pushed off, allowing Slaughterhouse to right himself almost instantaneously. Atomic Rex was still on the ground when Slaughterhouse lowered his forward facing head and rammed into the kaiju again. Slaughterhouse was pushing Atomic Rex along the ground as he attempted to gore the nuclear theropod.

Slaughterhouse's horns were just starting to penetrate Atomic Rex's scales when the saurian kaiju placed his powerful legs under the bovine monster's front head and pushed him away, causing the entire front portion of his body to shift forty-five degrees. With Slaughterhouse no longer directly facing him, Atomic Rex was able to return his body to an upright stance. Atomic Rex moved toward Slaughterhouse as the misshapen kaiju was turning back toward him. The two monsters were facing each other, and Chris watched them fight in close quarters. Atomic Rex's powerful arms clawed at the exposed muscles of Slaughterhouse while the fused creature used the horns on his front head to jab at the kaiju while the hooves on the top and sides of its body struck at Atomic Rex as well.

The two beasts continued to exchange blows in this fashion until Atomic Rex was able to dig his claws into the flesh underneath Slaughterhouse's bottom front legs. Atomic Rex lifted the front half of Slaughterhouse's body off the ground while at the same time stepping forward. Slaughterhouse mooed in frustration when he found himself standing upright on his back two lower legs. With Slaughterhouse standing completely on his back two lower legs, Atomic Rex took another step forward and pushed. He toppled over the mammalian the creature only to have the legs that were protruding out of its back land firmly on the ground. With two of its heads now upside down, Slaughterhouse's spun around and began swinging his forward head from side to side in an attempt to slash Atomic Rex's knees with its horns.

Atomic Rex backed away from Slaughterhouse, and when he did, the bovine horror threw his body to the right, landing on his side legs which continued his momentum so that his body righted itself again and all three of his heads were returned to their correct orientation. As Atomic Rex watched Slaughterhouse right his body, the nuclear theropod realized that the beast's extra legs were the location that he needed to attack. Atomic Rex roared as he charged the horrid monster. When he reached Slaughterhouse, Atomic Rex reached out with his claws and grabbed the horns of the front-facing head and stopped them from goring him.

Atomic Rex reached his massive jaws forward as the flailing legs atop of Slaughterhouse struck him on the head. Atomic Rex ignored the blows and sunk his teeth into the right front leg on Slaughterhouse's back. With one powerful turn of his neck, Atomic Rex tore the leg loose and threw it on the ground. He quickly repeated the move on the left leg front leg protruding from the monster's back. The saurian kaiju then pulled up on Slaughterhouse's horns once more, lifting the bovine creature's bottom front legs off the ground. Atomic Rex then tossed the bull-like monster's head to the side once more, causing it turn at a forty-five-degree angle.

The legs on the right side of Slaughterhouse's body were now directly in front of Atomic Rex. Atomic Rex latched onto one of the legs with his claws while closing his mouth on the other leg. Atomic Rex pulled on both of the legs and yanked them off Slaughterhouse's body. The injured Slaughterhouse attempted to move away from Atomic Rex, but the saurian kaiju dug his claws into the injured beast's right side and held him in place. The heads on Slaughterhouses back and his right side shook back and forth as they tried in vain to attack their adversary.

Atomic Rex roared at the head on the abominations right side. The nuclear theropod then plunged his clawed foot into the side head. Two of Atomic Rex's foot claw's punctured the eyes on the side head, blinding it. The blind head was mooing in pain until Atomic Rex raked his foot down across the rest of the head's face, slicing it to ribbons.

With his grip still firmly holding Slaughterhouse in place, Atomic Rex closed his jaws on the head sticking out of the monster's back. Rather than tearing the head off, Atomic Rex chewed on it like the hunk of raw meat that it was until the head stopped moving. As Atomic Rex pulled his mouth off the second head, the raw meat that once been a face sloughed out of his mouth.

What remained of Slaughterhouse was bucking widely, trying to free itself from Atomic Rex's grip, but the saurian kaiju was too strong for him to break away from. With no legs left on the right side of its body to catch it, Atomic Rex pulled Slaughterhouse to the ground. Slaughterhouse hit the ground with a loud thud that shook his entire body. Before Slaughterhouse could react, Atomic Rex placed his foot on the bovine's body and pinned him to the ground.

Slaughterhouse's eyes grew wide when he saw Atomic Rex looming above him. The legs on the left side of its body kicked and bucked in an attempt to fight off the carnivorous beast that was looming above him. Just as he had done to the right side of Slaughterhouse's body, Atomic Rex grabbed one of the side legs in his mouth and the other in his claws. Atomic Rex tore off the upper side leg with single pull while he twisted the lower side leg with his claws until it snapped and hung limply off Slaughterhouse's body. Sensing that death was near, Slaughterhouse bucked as hard as he could in an attempt to free himself from beneath Atomic Rex, but the bovine's motions only caused Atomic Rex's clawed toes to dig themselves deeper into his body. Atomic Rex roared one more time before leaning down and using his jaws to tear out Slaughterhouse's remaining head's jugular.

In the sky above the carnage, Chris watched as blood poured out of Slaughterhouse's jugular while the kaiju thrashed in its death throes. After a few seconds, the misshapen beast finally died. Atomic Rex didn't waste time announcing his victory to the world. He simply started to eat his kill, as did the swarm of flies that descended on their former host. Chris turned away from the horror below him. While he was glad that there was one less kaiju in the world had no desire to watch Atomic Rex ingest its remains. Chris set Steel Samurai 2.0 on autopilot so that it would hover well above Atomic Rex while he slept. He also set a motion detector so that he would know if Atomic Rex left the area. Chris knew that kaiju would stay right where he was, first to eat his kill, and then to re-engage the mech that was floating above him. Chris walked to the makeshift bed in the back of the cockpit where he laid down and quickly fell asleep, setting a timer to wake him up in four hours.

CHAPTER 16

NORTHERN PARAGUAY

Kate, Pablo, and Ruiz tried to catch a few hours of sleep inside of the truck, but with the heat, humidity, limited space, and insects pouring through the windows, it was difficult to get comfortable. Kate had grown up in the American southwest, so she was used to heat, but not the overwhelming humidity of the rainforest. Pablo and Ruiz had offered to sleep in the back of the truck and to take turns on watch for any giant mutants that might stumble by. Kate had the cabin of the truck to herself, and even without the discomforts of a cramped truck in the rainforest, sleep would have been difficult for Kate as she wondered about her husband, children, and the people who she was responsible for back in Washington. She knew that Chris was more than capable of handling himself, but she also knew that as much as she was trying to face her fears of Ogre in the form of Yetaiju, Chris was facing his facing his fears head on in Atomic Rex. She had seen Chris grow as a person in their time together, especially when he became a father. She resolved herself to contact him the next morning for an update on his mission and simply to hear his voice.

She had tried a few times to contact her children back at home to see how they were faring, as well as to see how the campsite was doing in her absence, but she was only able to pick up static when trying to contact the camp. Kate was confident that her children would be able to handle whatever issues they faced in the campsite in terms of external issues. Her only concern for her children was in dealing with the council if the need arose. Kate said a silent prayer for her family, and then she closed her eyes to catch a few hours of much-needed sleep.

When she awoke, Kate contacted Chris over the radio and they informed each other of their current positions. She was relieved that Chris had not only gotten Atomic Rex moving in a southern direction, but that he had spoken to the kids as well. Chris had suggested that the next time she talks to the kids that she do so using Morse code since there was some concern that the council members may have been scanning her communications for an opportunity to undercut her leadership. She thanked her husband, told him that she loved him, and then made a promise to herself to send the kids a message in Morse code as soon as possible. After Kate had finished communicating with Chris, Ruiz started up the truck, and he began looking for a spot where they could cross the river.

Revenant was wandering through the jungle, still searching for the humans whose faces were fixed in his mind. He was several miles south of the river when he heard the sound of the truck turning over. The kaiju growled as part of him remembered the sound of the truck and realized that the people he was looking for would be in the vehicle.

It took them roughly an hour of driving alongside the river before they were able to find an area that was shallow enough and had a firm enough bottom for them to cross the river with the truck. Once they had crossed with the truck, they followed the path on the other side of the river back toward the area that Yetaiju had crushed flat as he ran after the horses. Even with the trees crushed, the path that the yeti had created was not suitable for a truck. Ruiz was only able to push the vehicle at a little over ten miles per hour along the bumpy path, and even at that speed, he knew that the truck was being shaken apart.

He looked over toward Kate as she bounced up and down in the seat next him. "Without a clear path to drive on or the horses, we will never be able to outrun Yetaiju if he chases us again. What is our current course of action?"

Kate put her hand on the radio. "Our plan is still the same. We will track Yetaiju's movements, divert him away from your campsite as needed, and keep in touch with Chris as to our location so that he can lead Atomic Rex here. Chris is currently in Costa Rica. Atomic Rex has killed the kaiju known as Slaughterhouse, and Chris will continue luring the monster farther south into El Lobo Blanco's territory. "

The truck bounced hard over a fallen and partially crushed tree as Ruiz continued to question Kate about their current course of action. "What if we find Yetaiju? He will see and hear the truck as soon as we are near him, and without a road to drive on, Yetaiju will easily catch us." Ruiz shrugged. "That's even if the truck is still functional by the time we reach the monster."

Kate returned the man's shrug. "Ruiz, I don't know what else to tell you. I don't have an answer for every situation that we might come across. All that I do know is that it's our responsibility to do whatever we can to keep that monster away from your camp and to keep Chris updated on his position so he can lead Atomic Rex to Yetaiju, and hopefully, they will kill each other." Kate looked out the window at the path ahead of them. "On the bright side of things, the yeti seems to have chased the horses in a northeast direction. As long as he keeps moving in the opposite direction of your camp, then all we need to do is track his location for Chris."

Pablo turned his head toward both of them. "What if we were to look for Revenant? Is it possible that he can still assist in not only fighting Yetaiju but the other kaiju as well?"

Ruiz shook his head. "I fear that at this point, should we encounter Revenant again, that he will present a threat to us rather than a benefit." He was fighting back tears as he turned away from the other two. "Revenant is more monster than man now."

Kate and Pablo could see that Ruiz was upset. Kate placed her hand on Ruiz's shoulder. He smiled at her and nodded before returning his eyes to the makeshift path. The three people rode on in silence, unaware that Revenant was less than two miles behind them and gaining on them with each passing second.

Five miles northeast of the truck in southern Bolivia, Yetaiju was sleeping in the middle of the jungle. The giant yeti had captured the horses shortly after the humans had abandoned them. Angry that he had chased the animals for so long only find that the yeti-like creatures he sought were no longer with them, Yetaiju crushed the horses in his bare hands and devoured their remains. The beast searched the area for a short time in hopes of finding the Yeti-like creatures, but when he was unable to locate them, he decided that it was time for him to rest.

Yetaiju was dreaming of his former life in the frozen valley when a loud buzzing sound awoke him. The giant yeti sat up and looked around, but he was unable to determine where the sound had come from. Yetaiju heard the sound again coming from behind him, but when he turned around, he saw only the jungle.

In the clouds above Yetaiju, the kaiju known as Dragonus circled the sky as she eyed the beast which had invaded her territory. Dragonus had the overall form of a dragonfly with the notable exception of squid-like tentacles dangling below her body instead of legs. She watched as Yetaiju stood to his full height, and when he did, the winged kaiju swooped down to attack him.

Yetaiju heard the buzzing sound again; this time, it was in the sky above him. The yeti looked up to see the streaking blur that was Dragonus heading toward him. As Dragonus was approaching Yetaiju, she unsheathed the giant hooks that were embed within her tentacles. Dragonus swooped over Yetaiju dragging her tentacles over the primate's face, head, and shoulders as she flew by him. Yetaiju roared in pain as the effect of the attack was akin to having hundreds of razor blades propelled at his face by a hurricane.

Yetaiju could hear Dragonus in the sky above him as the insect kaiju turned around in the air and dove at him again. The yeti managed to throw his arms in front of his face and head a second before Dragonus reached him, resulting in the winged kaiju's tentacles raking Yetaiju's arms instead of his face. After her tentacles ran over Yetaiju's arms, Dragonus once again flew into the clouds.

As soon as Yetaiju felt the tentacles peel away from his arms, he bent down and started tearing trees up from the ground with both of his hands. When he saw Dragonus emerge from the clouds, Yetaiju began hurling the uprooted trees at the insect. To Yetaiju's surprise, the flying horror was easily able to dodge the projectiles. Dragonus flew over, under, and around the trees that Yetaiju threw at her as she streaked toward the primate. Despite Dragonus's incredible speed, the intelligent yeti was timing her attack. When Dragonus had covered nearly half the distance between them, Yetaiju started the motion of swinging his hand above his head. By the time that Dragonus was above Yetaiju's head, his hand had completed its swing. The yeti swatted the insect in the face and forced her to veer away from him.

Dragonus quickly circled around just above the tree line, and she flew at Yetaiju's back before the yeti had the chance to turn around. Dragonus pinned her body flat against Yetaiju's back, and she wrapped her tentacles around the yeti's torso. She then reared her head back and used her mouth to bite into Yetaiju's shoulders as her tentacles acted like huge pieces of barbed wire, tightening themselves around the yeti's torso.

Yetaiju howled in pain as Dragonus's tentacles sliced into him. The yeti fought through the pain and began using his hands to freeze the insect's tentacles in the fashion that he had against the lobster mutant he had fought several days ago. Dragonus's two main tentacles were quickly frozen solid. When Yetaiju realized this, he squeezed them and crushed the frozen appendages into dust. Dragonus started to pull away her remaining tentacles, which allowed Yetaiju the freedom to reach around and grab the giant insect's head. The yeti wrenched Dragonus's mouth off his shoulder, and then he pulled the insect in front of him.

Dragonus's wings started to vibrate as she tried to break Yetaiju's grip and fly away, but before she was able to, the yeti reached out and grabbed the wings on the right side of her body. Yetaiju roared, and then he ripped off Dragonus's right wings. Yetaiju let go of the insect, and he watched as Dragonus fell helpless to the ground in front of him. The insect continued to move her remaining wings in an attempt to take to the sky, but her efforts only resulted in her crawling in a circle. Yetaiju roared at the creature that had attacked him. He then lifted his massive foot and brought it crashing down onto Dragonus's head, crushing it to a pulp.

With his foe vanquished, the mighty yeti roared in triumph. He was surprised when he heard a women's scream in reply. Yetaiju quickly sniffed the air, and when he caught the scent of the creatures he was looking for and the stench of another monster, he ran off in the direction of the scream.

CHAPTER 17

WASHINGTON STATE

Emily and Kyle had quickly gathered what weapons, supplies, and people that they could to face the oncoming threat of Ramrod. The siblings' resources to face the giant mutant included twenty people, twelve men and eight females, a dozen rifles and shotguns, three flare guns, two binoculars, and ten gallons of gasoline.

The small firearms were predominately used for hunting deer and other game animals. Giant mutants were usually not completely indestructible like the True Kaiju, but Ramrod's skin and muscles were still far too dense for rifles and shotguns to injure him. Usually, this was not an issue for the camp because Chris and Steel Samurai 2.0 were able to deal with any threat posed by a giant mutant with relative ease. This time, there was no mech to protect the camp. This time, their father was not there to save everyone. The people of the camp were relying on Emily, Kyle, and their team to divert Ramrod, or at least to delay him long enough for them to evacuate the campsite.

The brother and sister team worked together to construct a plan for dealing with the quickly approaching threat. Once Kyle had taken an inventory of their supplies, he quickly reported it to his sister. With that information, Emily began to consider Ramrod's tendencies and how she could expose them with the resources she had to divert the mutant from his current path.

Emily looked at her brother. "For the most part, Ramrod it pretty skittish. He is more prone to be scared of something and run away from it rather than to attack it. That's what is going on now. Atomic Rex scared the hell out him, and he is just running over anything that he can to put as much distance between himself and Atomic Rex as possible." Emily pointed at the ten gallons of gasoline. "I had thought that we could use the gas cans as some kind of explosive weapon, but maybe they will work better as an accelerant to starting a big fire." She looked to her brother. "This is where we need that big brain of yours. On the path that Ramrod is currently heading, where is the best area where we can start a large forest fire?"

Kyle closed his eyes for a moment as he recalled the topography of the area Ramrod was running through. His eyes shot open as the idea of where to set the fire came into his head. He pulled out a map of the area and he pointed to a spot roughly fifty miles west of Portland. "Ramrod is essentially running up the coast. If he continues on that path, he will run through Orange Coast Range. Back in the 1930s, a series of bad forest fires occurred there. The people of the time called it the Tillamook Burn." He looked toward his sister. "If we can start a fire there, it will spread quickly. It's also far enough away from us that it won't present much of a danger to the campsite. The winds will blow the smoke to the south, and the flames would have to cross over one hundred and twenty miles and three rivers to reach us." He shrugged. "If there will be anything that will scare Ramrod off his current course, a large fire should do the job."

Emily nodded and turned to the group of people who were waiting for her to give commands. "Alright, let's go! It's about an hour travel time for us to reach the Orange Coast Range, which means that Ramrod should reach there almost at the exact same time that we do, so let's move it!"

The men and women jumped into five SUV's and took off out of the camp. As they were driving, Emily and Kyle discussed how to best start a large forest fire in a relatively small amount of time.

Kyle ran through all of the logistics of what they were going to do with his sister. "Our biggest issue is that we don't know exactly how Ramrod will navigate through the Coast Range. It's not like we can just pull up in front of him and start a fire to scare him off. Out best bet is to make our initial fire as widespread as possible. We have three flares and roughly ten gallons of gasoline. I suggest that we set three separate fires roughly five miles apart. The best way to accomplish this quickly will be to put brush around the bottom of trees, douse the brush in gasoline, run the gasoline from our starter tree to trees next to it, going in the direction of the next fire, and then to use the flare to start the fire."

Emily nodded. "Sounds good. So we will start at the northern edge of the forest to give us as much time as possible." She looked over at Charles who was driving the truck, and she was glad to see that he already had the vehicle moving at its top speed. She took a deep breath and directed her attention back to Kyle. "We are going to have to wait around as close to the fire as we can to see if diverts Ramrod or not."

Kyle nodded. "We can take the highway most of the way there, spread out when we reach the forest, and then regroup on the highway north of where we start the fire so that the wind will blow the smoke away from us." He pointed to a section of highway on the map. "There is a section of the highway here that is at the top of a large hill. From the top of it, you can see for miles in any direction. With our binoculars, we should be able to see Ramrod when he enters the forest, but what do we do if the fire doesn't alter his course?"

Emily shrugged at looked at her rifle. "We take what weapons we have, and we try to use them to make him change his direction."

Kyle gave his sister a slightly sarcastic smile. "We had better hope that the fire scares him."

The team made good time reaching the targeted area. Emily put Charles and Sean in charge of the first team. She knew that despite being only thirteen, Charles had a good head on his shoulders and would follow directions. Sean was as strong as an ox and would move as much brush into place as possible, simply to try and impress her. She took note of how effective her tactics of enticing the young man were proving to be. She watched as the team departed from their SUV's and sprinted into the trees. Emily saw Charles barking out orders to Sean and the other team members as they started to gather brush and pile it up around the base of a tall tree.

The team made it to the next drop area in under two minutes. Kyle and his friends, Mike and Carmello, along with two others, quickly went to work on setting up the second site. Emily was watching through the rearview window of the SUV as it pulled away and she whispered, "Good luck, little brother." Emily then grabbed her rifle and slung it over her back as she prepared herself to lead the team at the last targeted site.

Less than two minutes later, Emily's team reached their target site. As soon as she opened the door to the vehicle, she started shouting out orders. She pointed to a large tree, "That's tree zero for us; we are going to build up the kindling around it. Look for dried twigs, leaves, and dead branches. Anything that will burn quickly and be easy to move. We are lighting this fire in five minutes, so let's make this thing happen!" As they were working, the smell of burning trees wafted through the night air. Emily smiled and said to her team, "It smells like team one was successful in starting their fire! Keep moving! We have three minutes to start our fire!" She was pulling a clump of dried leaves over to tree zero when a loud growled echoed through the woods.

Everyone immediately stopped working and starting looking around the woods to see what had made the sound. Emily quickly pulled her rifle off her back and looked into the pitch-black woods. She could see that her team was scared, but she needed them to keep working. She shouted, "It's a wild cat! The animal is probably scared by the fire that teams one and two have started! Just keep working! The sooner that we get the fire started, the safer we will be from animal attacks!"

Her team quickly went into a blur of action, gathering as much twigs and brush as they could and placing it around the base of tree zero. Emily quietly walked over in the direction that the roar had come from. She had been out hunting with her father countless times growing up. With the decline of the human race, many of the animal species that were facing extinction were now starting to make a comeback and cougars were at the top of that list. Emily knew a cougar roar when she heard one, and if the animal was making that much noise when it was close to potential prey, she knew that the beast was desperate. She could hear movement in the trees and she yelled to her team, "Quickly, pour the gasoline on the brush! We need to get out of here!"

Two young men ran over to the truck, grabbed the gasoline, and then ran over to the brush around the base of tree zero. Emily was watching them closely as they walked toward the tree, and when she saw the slightest movement in the woods behind them, she immediately fired her gun. There was another loud roar, and Emily was sure that she had injured the cougar but not killed it. She yelled to the two young men, "Run for the SUV, now!"

The two men bolted for the SUV, and they had no sooner taken off than the cougar jumped out of the woods toward them. Just as her father had taught her, Emily dropped to one knee and took her time aiming at the animal. She took a slow breath and squeezed the trigger rather than pulling it as an amateur would have. Her bullet struck the cougar directly in the chest and the beast dropped to the ground dead. The people who were in the SUV cheered for Emily, and she allowed herself a brief smile at their admiration. She then darted to the SUV, jumped into the passenger side, closed the door, rolled down the window, and yelled for the driver to take off. As they were speeding away, she leaned out the window and fired the flare gun at tree zero. When the flare landed at the base of the tree, it exploded in a bright orange plume.

Emily and her team drove in a northern direction away from the flames before heading back toward the highway to avoid the fires started by the other two teams. As they made their way back toward the highway, Emily could see the inferno growing as it spread through the forest. She hated to see so much beautiful woodland go up in flames, but she kept reminding herself that it was the only way that she could save her home and the people who lived there. Fifteen minutes later, she met Kyle's and Charles's teams on top of the hill where they were going to watch as Ramrod approached the blaze. The fire was well over ten miles wide now. Emily was using her binoculars to scan the eastern side of the fire while Kyle scanned the western side of it. Each of them was silently hoping that the fire had spread far enough to impede Ramrod's path.

Ten minutes that felt like several hours to Emily passed before she saw Ramrod appear on the horizon. She shouted, "I see him!"

Kyle replied, "Well, at least we know that he will encounter the fire. Now let's just hope that it's enough to scare him off."

The brother and sister watched through their binoculars as Ramrod approached the flames. Kyle described the mutants movements to the rest of team who could only make out the giant ram as a dot on the horizon. "He's slowing down as he is getting closer to the fire." Kyle was silent for a moment before continuing, "He is rearing up at the flames and moving backward on his hind legs." Kyle was silent again for a few seconds before he screamed, "He's turning around! He is running away from the flames! We did it!"

The rest of the gathered team cheered, and they began shaking hands and hugging each other. Emily first called out over her radio for Erica and Fred, who were still tracking Ramrod, to head east to avoid the fire and then to return to camp.

She then hugged Kyle, and when she released him, she turned around to see Sean staring at her with a big stupid smile on his face. He shook his head. "You are amazing, Emily. You saved the entire camp."

She smiled back at him. "It was a team effort, and we couldn't have done it without your help."

Sean leaned in a little closer to her. "Does that mean that I earned more than a kiss on the cheek?"

Emily looked at the muscle-bound man in front of her. She knew that he was not the most intelligent man in the camp, but even she had to admit that he was attractive. She said out loud, "What the hell. Why not?" She shrugged, and then she grabbed Sean by the neck and passionately kissed him.

CHAPTER 18

SOUTHERN COSTA RICA

Chris's alarm went off, waking him up. He walked over to the pilot's seat of Steel Samurai 2.0. The mech was still hovering high in the air above the carcass of Slaughterhouse. He looked down and was surprised to see that Atomic Rex had moved on and his motion alarm had not gone off. He guessed that the motion alarm must have been damaged, and then he did a quick search on his computer for any nuclear power plants in the area. He was surprised to see that there was a plant fifty miles to the south in Panama. Chris laughed, "Well, isn't that nice. If Atomic Rex headed for the nuclear power plant, then he is already heading into El Lobo Blanco's territory." Chris tried briefly to contact Emily and Kyle using Morse code, but he didn't get any response. He also tried to quickly contact Kate, but he was unable to reach her either.

Chris sighed and said to himself, "They are all perfectly fine. They're just not able to respond right this second." Chris closed his eyes and refocused his thoughts on the task at hand, and then he started flying south into Panama.

Atomic Rex could feel the power of the nuclear reactor calling to him. After feasting on the remains of both Behemoth and Slaughterhouse, he felt more satiated than he had in years. He had eaten more meat in the past two days than he had in the previous six months. His body had more than enough food in it to sustain him for at least a week before he needed to feed again.

While his body had its fill of meat, his battles with the creatures he had eaten as well as his encounter with Steel Samurai 2.0 had diminished the nuclear energy stored within his body. The kaiju could feel the radiation leaking out of the destroyed nuclear power plant that was just ahead of him. He body was already soaking up the ambient radiation from the plant, and while it was slowly recharging him, the monster needed to access the reactor at the core of the plant to fully recharge himself.

Atomic Rex was less than two miles from the plant when he stopped walking and sniffed the air. He was in a valley surrounded by large hills, and while he couldn't see anything around him that would pose a challenge, his keen sense of smell detected the scent of another kaiju. Atomic Rex looked at the hills around him and roared a challenge at the unseen threat that was stalking him. A reply came in the sound of a loud guttural howl that was followed by hundreds of other howls.

Atomic Rex looked to his left in the direction of the loudest howl. He saw a large furry white form creep around the edge of the nearest hill. The beast had a long canine-like snout with teeth protruding from both its upper and lower jaws. The kaiju had burning bright yellow eyes and large white pointed ears.

The creature was roughly one hundred and forty feet tall at the shoulder blade. The beast was bipedal, but its posture was hunched over, giving it a gait and a stance similar to that of a gorilla. Its lower legs were curved away from the rest of its body, causing the creature to mostly walk with its arms and hands supporting its torso. The beast had a large white tail that curved off the back end of its body. As El Lobo Blanco moved out from behind the hills, hundreds of other wolves, each roughly thirty feet high, emerged from hills that surrounded Atomic Rex. El Lobo Blanco was the alpha male and leader of the pack of giant mutant wolves.

El Lobo Blanco howled again and the hundreds of mutant wolves that were standing on the hills charged Atomic Rex. The wolves were only about one-fourth the size of the nuclear theropod, but they attacked as a pack. Dozens of mutant wolves were biting and clawing at Atomic Rex's feet and legs. The saurian kaiju fought back against the pack with the fury that carried him to victory over countless other kaiju. Atomic Rex reached down and snatched up three of the mutant wolves in his jaws, killing them instantly. He tossed the corpses of three wolves aside, and then he reached down and bit into two more mutants. The nuclear theropod used his long powerful claws to strike at the wolves in front of him while simultaneously swiping his tail from side to side to knock down the wolves attacking him from behind.

Atomic Rex was killing off everyone mutant wolf that he saw, but the sheer number of the pack of mutated animals was starting overwhelm him. Despite his efforts, the mutant wolves were continuing to maul his feet and legs. Some of the animals had even managed to latch onto his forearms or to jump onto his back. Atomic Rex was slowly being ripped to pieces.

Atomic Rex's body was covered in mutant wolves when he raised his head to the sky and roared. The wolves that were attached to Atomic Rex's body began to yelp in pain as the nuclear power stored within the kaiju's cells began to emanate from his body. Several of the wolves jumped off Atomic Rex, and they tried to run away from the kaiju, only to be blocked by their brethren who were still waiting to attack the saurian monster. Atomic Rex lifted his right foot off the ground, and when he brought it crashing back to the Earth, the Atomic Wave exploded from his body. Hundreds of mutant wolves were sent flying through the air as the blue dome of energy expanded outward from Atomic Rex.

El Lobo Blanco saw the blast coming toward him, and he quickly moved behind a hill to protect himself from the attack. El Lobo Blanco held his body close to the ground behind the hill and he watched as the blue energy cascaded over his head. When the energy dissipated, El Lobo Blanco moved out from behind the hill and that was when he saw his entire pack laying charred and dead at the feet of Atomic Rex. The smell of burnt fur hung in the air as El Lobo Blanco unleashed a howl of anguish and mourning at the loss of his pack.

Chris could see the Atomic Wave from miles away. He flew directly toward it, and when he saw Atomic Rex standing in the middle of an army of charred mutant wolves, he laughed. "If only Atomic Rex would find each of the other kaiju on his own, my job would be a lot easier." He then had Steel Samurai 2.0 hold a position roughly a mile away from the fight. When he saw El Lobo Blanco growling at Atomic Rex, he leaned back in his chair. "Time for the main event, I suppose."

Atomic Rex and El Lobo Blanco were staring at each other over the pack of dead mutant wolves. The giant wolf did not roar or howl, he simply sprang at Atomic Rex. Atomic Rex was caught off guard as El Lobo Blanco crashed into him and wrapped his arm around him. Atomic Rex was forced back a few steps as El Lobo Blanco pushed him backward and bit into his shoulder.

Atomic Rex ignored the pain in his shoulder and then wrapped his own arms around the kaiju wolf. The two monsters grappled for a few seconds before Atomic Rex was able to toss El Lobo Blanco to the ground. The wolf hit the ground and rolled away from Atomic Rex before the saurian beast was able to capitalize on grounding his opponent. El Lobo Blanco sprung behind Atomic Rex and then grabbed the base of Atomic Rex's tail with his claws and clamped his teeth down on the end of the nuclear theropod's tail.

Atomic Rex tried to reach into his cells to force the wolf beast off him with another blast of his Atomic Wave. Atomic Rex was surprised when he realized that his cells had not yet recharged to the point where he could unleash another Atomic Wave. The saurian kaiju roared, and then pulled his tail forward with such force that he wrenched El Lobo Blanco off his tail and sent the mammalian creature rolling across the ground in front of him.

Atomic Rex ran over to El Lobo Blanco. Once more, the white wolf moved like a flash of lightning as he lifted his head off the ground and sank his teeth into Atomic Rex's ankle. Atomic Rex roared in pain and then delivered three kicks to El Lobo Blanco's ribs which forced the wolf-beast to release his foot. El Lobo Blanco rolled way from Atomic Rex and regained his feet. Atomic Rex was preparing to charge his opponent when El Lobo Blanco sprang at him again. The two monsters became a blur of teeth, claws, fur, and scales as they tore into each other. Neither of the two kaiju was gaining an upper hand until Atomic Rex wrapped his arms around the wolf beast and threw it to the ground.

Chris continued to watch the battle from Steel Samurai 2.0. He was analyzing the fight as it unfolded before him. "Atomic Rex isn't used to fighting a monster quicker than he is. He is going to have to switch up his tactics if he wants to win this fight."

The analysis had no sooner left Chris's lips than Atomic Rex took several steps backward. El Lobo Blanco sprang toward him again, but the adaptable Atomic Rex was ready for the attack. El Lobo Blanco was still in the air when Atomic Rex spun around and used his tail to swat the wolf monster away. Rather than waiting for El Lobo Blanco to stop rolling from the strike, Atomic Rex charged after the monster while he was still in motion. When El Lobo Blanco stopped his motion and was preparing to right himself for another attack, Atomic Rex was already on him. The nuclear theropod closed his jaws around the upper part of El Lobo Blanco's left arm. Atomic Rex pulled and chewed on the arm while using his claws to tear into the socket that connected the arm to El Lobo Blanco's body. There was a sickening tearing sound as Atomic Rex ripped El Lobo Blanco's arm out of its socket.

El Lobo Blanco limped away from Atomic Rex as he howled in pain. The wolf beast was trying to flee when Atomic Rex charged the monster and closed his powerful jaws on El Lobo Blanco's head. The saurian kaiju's lower teeth shattered the wolf's jaw while his upper teeth penetrated El Lobo Blanco's skull and pierced his brain. El Lobo Blanco's body twitched for several seconds before it finally stopped moving.

When he was sure that his adversary was deceased, Atomic Rex released the monster from his jaws. El Lobo Blanco's body fell to the ground, surrounded by the other dead members of his pack. With his opponent defeated, Atomic Rex turned and started walking toward the nuclear reactor.

Chris was watching the injured and exhausted Atomic Rex walking toward the reactor. He knew that it was unlikely that he would have a better chance than he did right now of slaying Atomic Rex. Steel Samurai 2.0 was operating at one hundred percent, and the mech was far faster and stronger than it was the last time he had tried to kill Atomic Rex. Chris thought that all he would need to do was fly at Atomic Rex at top speed and drive Steel Samurai's 2.0 sword into the kaiju's neck. He knew that if the blow didn't outright decapitate the monster that it would least incapacitate him to the point where he could kill him.

The thought of putting an end to the kaiju was tempting to Chris, and while he knew that Steel Samurai 2.0 could kill an injured Atomic Rex, he also knew that he could not slay the other uninjured monsters. He knew that he would need Atomic Rex to slay Liopleviathan and most importantly to slay Yetaiju so that Kate could return home with him, and so that his children would never have to live as a monster's pet.

Chris watched as Atomic Rex walked over to the nuclear reactor and began siphoning energy from it. Chris sneered. "Recharge and heal yourself, monster, because you still have a lot of battles ahead of you."

CHAPTER 19

NORTHERN PARAGUAY

Revenant could smell the people that he was looking for just ahead of him. The kaiju had tracked his prey for over thirty miles and had finally reached them. The kaiju crossed the river again, and as he did so, he could see the truck that held his prey making its way through a destroyed section of forest. The sight of his prey sent the monster into a frenzy. His compulsion to find these creatures was driving him insane. The monster roared then darted down the path after the truck containing his creator.

The truck continued to slowly make its way over the crushed trees that Yetaiju had left in his wake. The sun was shining directly into the cabin, making the already sweltering hot truck even more unbearable. Ruiz was driving, and he was starting to worry that the axles on the vehicle would break from the constant bouncing over knocked-down trees, but as walking was their only other alternative, he kept his concerns to himself. Pablo was sleeping in the middle seat between Ruiz and Kate. Kate was sitting on the passenger side of the truck and staring out the window. The three of them were still covered in dried mud from their last run in with Yetaiju, and with the heat inside the cabin of the truck, the three of them were extremely uncomfortable and they smelled horrible.

Kate was holding onto the radio and thinking about trying to contact her family again when they heard a roar from behind them. Pablo immediately woke up and Kate's head turned toward Ruiz. "That wasn't Yetaiju."

Ruiz shook his head. "No, it was Revenant." The scientist shrugged. "Maybe he has regained some of his mental acuity. Perhaps he is trying to catch up to us to protect us?"

Kate glanced at her side view mirror to see the deformed monster running directly toward them. There was no semblance of cognition or humanity in Revenant's face. She could clearly see that any part of him that was human was gone. She could also see the wild desire in the monster's eyes to catch them. It was the same look she had seen in Ogre's eyes all of those years ago when that demon held her prisoner. She yelled at Ruiz, "Push the truck as fast as you can!"

Ruiz tried to increase the truck's speed, but it only caused the vehicle to shake even more as it went over the rough terrain. He looked at Kate. "I can't go any faster. If I do, the truck will shake to pieces."

Kate glanced back at her side view mirror, and she realized that they had less than a minute until Revenant would reach them. Kate screamed, "Stop the truck and run into the jungle! Our only hope is to lose him in the trees!"

Ruiz immediately stopped the truck, jumped out the driver side door, and took off into the jungle in a western direction. Kate grabbed the portable radio, then she and Pablo ran out of the truck in a northeastern direction.

Revenant could see the humans running out of the truck, and while he felt compelled to kill all of them, it was the man who had run out by himself that the kaiju had the greatest desire to kill. Revenant swerved to his left as he chased Ruiz into the jungle.

Ruiz was sprinting as fast as he could through the jungle. Trees and bushes were cutting every inch of his body as he ran past them. He heard another roar, and he felt the ground shaking beneath him as he ran. He quickly came to the realization that Revenant had decided to chase him down rather than first going after the others. Ruiz's mind was overwhelmed with the possible implications of what that meant. Did Revenant feel the need to kill him for some internal reason? Was there still a part of Roberto in the kaiju's mind that blamed him for being a monster?

Ruiz's thoughts were cut short when Revenant stepped in front of him and forced Ruiz to stop running. Ruiz looked up at the monster he had created from the remains of a man. He could see not only the animalistic urge to kill in the monster's face but also a specific hatred that was directed at him. Revenant could simply have stepped on him and ended his life, but some part of the monster wanted Ruiz to see him.

At that moment, Ruiz knew he was going to die. He decided that if this was going to be the end of his life at the hands of his creation that he would at least meet his own maker with a clear conscious.

Ruiz looked up at his monster, and for the first time, he addressed him by his human name. "Roberto, I don't know if you can still understand me, but I have to say this. I am sorry for what I did to you. I know it would have been easier for you to die on the battlefield rather than to become a monster. No one should ever have been put through the hell that you have experienced."

Ruiz began to cry. "Having said that, given a second chance, I would have done it all the same way! It is only because of you that our people are alive after all of these years! If I have to pay with my life for the sins I have committed against you, then I accept that consequence with the knowledge that…" Ruiz's speech was cut short as Revenant reached down and snatched his creator off the ground.

Ruiz's speech was meaningless to Revenant. The man who was once Roberto was completely gone. All that remained of him was the echo of his last thoughts to find Ruiz and Kate. Revenant took one brief look at Ruiz, and then he crushed him in the palm of his hand. The movement was quick and Ruiz felt no pain. One second, he was looking into the eyes of his creation, and the next moment, he ceased to exist. Revenant didn't roar or give any other indication that he had accomplished a goal. He simply started running in a northeastern direction after Kate.

Pablo and Kate were racing through the jungle, trying to put as much distance between themselves and Revenant as they could. Kate had gotten a good look at the monster's eyes. This was not the typical kaiju that sought to defend his territory or to crush an invader. This monster had the mind of a trained killer on a mission, and his current mission was to kill her and Pablo.

As Kate ran, she looked for anything that could hide them from Revenant, but there was simply nothing to be found. She and Pablo could feel the ground shaking beneath them as Revenant grew closer to them with each step. Kate could hear trees being crushed behind them beneath the pounding footfalls of Revenant as he chased them with the tenacity of a bloodhound. They had only made it a little over half a mile from the truck when Revenant's foot came crashing down in front of them. Pablo and Kate looked at each other for a moment, and then Revenant shifted his clawed foot in the young man's direction. Pablo turned to run, and in the split second it took him to turn around, Revenant's talon shot out from his foot and burst through Pablo's chest. Revenant lifted his foot with the dying Pablo still impaled on it. Kate could see the pain in Pablo's eyes, and she screamed at the horror she was witnessing. Revenant kicked out his foot, which sent Pablo's corpse flying over the jungle. The giant then turned toward Kate with his mind still focused on killing her.

Kate ran to her left trying to get as much tree cover between herself and Revenant's line of vision as possible. When she ran into the trees, she fell into the abandoned burrow of some large animal. The burrow was just big enough to hide Kate underground when she pulled her knees into her chest. She was able to peer out of the burrow, and she hoped to see Revenant running past her into the woods, but instead, she saw the monster standing above her and looking down. The kaiju was not looking directly at her, but Kate was sure that he knew she was still in the area. Revenant reached his hand down, and he began running it across the ground knocking over trees as he searched for his prey. Kate was sure that it would only be a matter of time before he found her.

She was doing her best to hide her body inside of the burrow when she saw Revenant's hand buried several feet deep in the ground. His fingers were tearing the soil apart like a giant bulldozer as they moved toward her. Kate was faced with the options of being crushed by the kaiju's fingers and dying, or jumping out of her hiding space and buying herself a few more seconds of life to figure out her next step.

Opting for the slim chance of life, Kate pulled herself out of the burrow and dove out of the way of Revenant's hand. The kaiju's giant fingers missed Kate by less than ten feet as she ran farther into the jungle. Revenant saw his prey dart, and he was about to run after it when both he and Kate felt the ground shaking beneath them.

Kate stopped running in the direction she had been heading when the impact tremors she was feeling gave her an unmistakable sign that another kaiju was heading toward her. She then heard Yetaiju's now-familiar roar. Kate moved to the side so that the giant yeti wouldn't crush her as he ran through the jungle. Kate found a tree that was clear of Yetaiju's path and she ducked down behind it.

Revenant saw the other kaiju coming from far away, and while he felt the urge to kill Kate, he also still felt the urge to slay other kaiju. Revenant stood up and charged the approaching Yetaiju.

Kate watched as the two monsters grabbed each other by the throat and shoulders. Yetaiju stepped forward, and with one shove, he pushed Revenant off his feet and sent him flying through the air. Kate shook her head at Yetaiju's sheer physical power. Any doubts that she had as to who the stronger of the two kaiju was had been answered with one move by the giant yeti.

Revenant crashed into the jungle and rolled over twice before he was able to stop his momentum. The misshapen monster quickly stood up and charged Yetaiju. When he reached the yeti, Revenant struck Yetaiju with two quick blows to the head that, to Kate's astonishment, seemed to have no effect on the yeti. Yetaiju stepped forward and drove a hammer strike into Revenant's neck and shoulder that sent the monster crashing face first into the ground.

When Revenant hit the ground at Yetaiju's feet, he quickly rolled onto his back and thrust his clawed toe at the yeti's midsection. The claw cut Yetaiju across his waist, but it was unable to penetrate the giant yeti's thick abdominal muscles. Revenant's attack was painful to Yetaiju, but it was unable to do any harm to the primate. Yetaiju roared at Revenant then grabbed the monster by the right arm and leg. In another display of his awesome strength, Yetaiju lifted Revenant over his head, and then slammed him to the ground with the force of a small earthquake.

Revenant tried to sit up, but the broken bones in his ribs and legs forced him to lay back down on the jungle floor. He looked up to see Yetaiju jump on top of his chest and crush what was left of his ribcage. Revenant saw Yetaiju lift his fist into the air and the last thing his eyes beheld was the primate's fist coming toward his head. There was a sickening splatter as Yetaiju's fist crushed Revenant's skull. Despite the fact that he had killed Revenant with his first blow, the yeti delivered six more strikes to the corpse of his dead opponent before he was finished. With Revenant dead, Yetaiju threw his arms out at his sides and roared, proclaiming his victory to the world. Yetaiju then sniffed the air and looked directly at Kate.

Kate's immediate reaction was to run when Yetaiju looked at her, but she knew that trying to flee would have been a futile effort. She remembered both her time with Ogre and the stories her great aunt had told her. When it came to dealing with a beast that wanted to capture you, the best thing to do was to submit to him. Despite her fears, Kate took a step toward Yetaiju. She then knelt down in front of the kaiju, showing him that she was submissive to his will.

Yetaiju reached down and scooped up Kate in his hand. He was careful not to freeze the tiny creature as he had done to the other one. The giant yeti sniffed the creature, and he was pleased to discover that this newest creature was a woman. He looked at her carefully. She was not a yeti, but still, whatever this creature was, she and the others like her were the closest living thing that he had found to his own kind since he left the valley.

As he was staring at Kate, for the first time since he had awoken to find his entire world changed, Yetaiju felt a brief second of peace. He felt as if he had taken the first step in satisfying his desire to have some form of a family. As the thought of a family crossed his mind, he remembered Armorsaur and his desire to slay the wretched creature. He carefully held the newest member of his family in his hand as he continued to follow Armorsaur's scent in a northeastern direction.

Kate took several deep breaths to calm her nerves, and then she turned on her radio. "Chris, come in; this is Kate. Yetaiju has me in his possession, and it seems that he has killed the other members of my party. For the moment, I am safe and we are heading in the northeast direction. The monster is more powerful than we thought. He has killed several kaiju with relative ease, including Revenant. There is no way that you and Steel Samurai 2.0 could defeat him. I am sure that only Atomic Rex or a kaiju who was strong enough to kill him has a chance against Yetaiju." She paused to carefully consider her next words before she said them to the man she loved. "Do not come for me. Continue to stick to your plan. Use the kaiju to clear out a path so the people in the Peruvian settlement can head north before Liopleviathan returns. I am not sure how Yetaiju will react if he hears noise coming from the radio, so do not initiate contact with me. I will update you as often as I can." She looked away from the monster that was carrying her as she delivered the last part of her message. "I love you, Chris, and we will be together again soon."

CHAPTER 20

GULF OF PANAMA

It had been three hours since Chris last had received a communication from his wife. She was currently in the clutches of a giant yeti who was keeping her prisoner. Chris remembered how emotionally scarred Kate's psyche was after all of the years she had spent as Ogre's captive. Five years after the death of Ogre, she would still wake up screaming in the middle of the night. When Kate had told him she had been captured by the beast, his immediate instinct was to fly to her and try and rescue her from the clutches of the monster. Kate knew him well enough to know that rescuing her would be what he felt compelled to do, so she told him not to come for her and to stick to the plan. The plan that called for him to draw Atomic Rex into battle with three more kaiju before drawing him, or whatever kaiju was left standing, into a confrontation with Yetaiju.

Chris wanted nothing more than to forget about the plan and to fly to his wife's rescue, but he also knew if he did that, Kate would never forgive him. The fact that the yeti had captured her only confirmed her fears that the beast was seeking to take humans as his prisoners. Kate was fixated on the idea that her children would never have to live as the prisoners of a man-beast like she did. She was willing to die to prevent that from happening.

One of the few things that was helping Chris to remain calm and to focus on his mission was the recent report he had received from Emily and Kyle. Not only had they successfully evacuated the town, but they had also diverted an attack from the rampaging Ramrod. Even more than saving the town and the people in it, Emily had stood up to the leader of the Council Elders and threatened him to start putting the concerns of the people in the camp before his own. Chris had long followed Kate's diplomatic lead in dealing with the council, even though he thought that they needed to be dealt with in a more aggressive manner. Emily had finally done what Kate didn't want to do and he didn't know how to do. She put the council leader in his place and managed to get him to at least partially be the leader the people needed him to be. He couldn't have been prouder of her or Kyle for his role in helping to devise and execute the plans they had put into motion.

Kate was worried that Emily and Kyle could one day find themselves as prisoners of Yetaiju or dead under the feet of Atomic Rex. Chris had faith that neither one of those outcomes would ever come fruition. For as wonderful and intelligent as Kate was, she was blinded by her instinct as a mother to protect her children. Chris could see it, though. He could see that being raised in a world ruled by monsters had made their children far better adapted to survive in it than he and Kate ever would be. Emily and Kyle would find a way to survive in this world because it was the only world they had ever known.

When the kaiju had first appeared, Kate was a college student and Chris was a pilot for the most powerful air force in the world. Neither one of them knew what it meant to live in world with kaiju. They had to learn how strong they could be in such a world by overcoming adversities they had never dreamed of encountering. Emily and Kyle had grown up facing these adversities as an everyday fact of life, and because of that, they were far better equipped to deal with the world as it was than their parents could ever have hoped to be. Chris smiled at the thought of his children proving that they could not only survive in this world but thrive in it.

Chris's mind was brought back to what he was doing when he saw the coastline of Colombia ahead of him. He quickly checked his radar, and he was glad to see that despite the speed he was flying over the water, Atomic Rex was still right behind him. He had originally planned to have Atomic Rex exit Panama and enter South America through Venezuela where Chris was going to lead him into a battle with Innsmouth. Once he had learned that Kate had been captured by Yetaiju, Chris made some risky but hopefully time-saving adjustments to his plan.

First, he would lead Atomic Rex into Colombia to the territory of the seven-headed serpent known as Anacondoid. Once Atomic

Rex was engaged in battle with Anacondoid, Chris would fly Steel Samurai 2.0 at top speed into Innsmouth's territory where he would engage the monster and lead him into a confrontation with the winner of the Atomic Rex-Anacondoid battle.

Chris flew over the coast of Colombia and toward the interior of the county. Anacondoid was known to mainly stay in the rainforest section of the country close to the tributary rivers that feed into the Amazon River. Chris turned Steel Samurai 2.0 around to see Atomic Rex running after him. It was obvious to Chris that he still had the kaiju's attention, but he was frustrated, and one of the few things that he could do to make himself feel better was to use Atomic Rex as a punching bag in order to ensure that the monster continued to follow him. Chris aimed several of his high-powered rifles at the monster, and then he unleashed their fury on the nuclear theropod.

Atomic Rex roared in anger as the stinging bullets bounced off his indestructible scales and fell to the ground. The metal giant continued to attack him and Atomic Rex was determined to end its existence. Atomic Rex lowered his head and doubled his speed as he ran toward Steel Samurai 2.0. With Atomic Rex running at over one hundred and forty miles per hour, Chris set Steel Samurai 2.0 on course for the Amazon region of Colombia.

Pacific Ocean

With a length of over seventy feet from head to tail, the mutated barracuda was one of the deadliest predators in the ocean. There were few creatures that it was not able to hunt and to kill. The barracuda was an apex predator who had never met his equal in terms of size, speed, strength, or ferocity. Still, as the mutant fish cruised through the water, it was terrified of what was below it. The mutant didn't have a mind capable of processing the information its senses were feeding it. All that the barracuda had to guide his actions were instincts and currently its instincts were telling the mutant that he was being hunted. The giant mutant nervously shifted his body from side to side as he felt that whatever was hunting him was closing in. The barracuda panicked and darted through the water at a speed that few other creatures could match.

Despite the speed at which he was moving, the giant barracuda could still see something moving up from the depths below him and gaining on him. The panicked fish quickly change his course and swerved to the left, but its efforts were in vain. The creature hunting the barracuda was far faster than the mutant fish.

Liopleviathan darted up from the depths behind and below the fleeing barracuda. The gargantuan sea beast closed his massive jaws over the seventy-foot mutant and swallowed it in a single bite. The relatively small meal did little to satisfy the sea monster's hunger. The oversized kaiju rose to the surface of the water. When he broke the surface of the Pacific, he looked like an island rising from the depths of the ocean. Liopleviathan roared, and then he started swimming in the direction of South America in search of more food.

Rainforest Region of Panama

Chris had Steel Samurai 2.0 hold a position in the air over the marshy swamp below him. He had his radar on, and it was reading multiple large targets in the area. Chris knew that the one target roughly two miles behind him and closing fast was Atomic Rex. He also knew that the other targets he was reading were most likely large mutants but not the kaiju he was looking for. Like most serpents, Anacondoid preferred to stay close to the ground and underwater. The kaiju was extremely difficult to locate. Chris wouldn't be able to simply find Anacondoid on radar and lead Atomic Rex right to him. Chris was going to have to keep Atomic Rex in the heart of Anacondoid's territory until the serpentine kaiju showed up to defend his domain.

Chris landed Steel Samurai 2.0 then looked out through his visual feed at the northern horizon. He only had to wait a few minutes before Atomic Rex started to come into view. The kaiju was truly amazing. Atomic Rex had swum the length of the Gulf of Panama and then had sprinted across most of Colombia, and the monster was still ready for battle.

Chris quickly checked his remaining ammunition. He had been very judicious with the use of his long-range weapons, and he still had plenty of high-caliber bullets and missiles left. He knew that he still had an encounter with Liopleviathan ahead of him. The encounter with the sea beast was what he was saving the majority of his ammunition for since even Steel Samurai 2.0 was not large enough to injure the monster in a physical confrontation. Chris decided that it was worth the risk to again engage Atomic Rex with a hit-and-run tactic and hope that would be able to disengage from the monster and reach a safe distance without sustaining heavy damage or dying.

Atomic Rex continued to walk deeper into the marsh toward the hovering mech. When the monster was roughly a half mile from Steel Samurai 2.0, Chris flew the mech directly at the kaiju with the hope of tackling Atomic Rex to the ground and landing several blows before taking off again and drawing the monster deeper into Anacondoid's territory.

Atomic Rex saw Steel Samurai 2.0 streaking toward him, and the kaiju recalled the previous time that the mech had used this tactic. The kaiju knew the mech was going to crash into him, and then once again run away. The kaiju roared and reached deep into his cells to call forth a portion of the power he had absorbed. His scales began to give off a blue glow as Steel Samurai 2.0 continued to fly toward him.

Chris saw Atomic Rex charging for his Atomic Wave at the last possible second. He pulled up hard on Steel Samurai's controls, and the mech shot up into the sky like a rocket as the blue dome of nuclear energy exploded from Atomic Rex's body. Chris knew that he was too close to Atomic Rex when the Atomic Wave was unleashed to outrun it. All that he could do was ride the wave to its apex and hope that by moving with the blast, he could limit the damage to his mech.

It was only a second after he had pulled up that the Atomic Wave struck Steel Samurai 2.0. The entire cockpit was rocked, and it tumbled through the air as the Atomic Wave pushed the mech higher into the sky. The cockpit was spinning around Chris as Steel Samurai 2.0 lost control of its flight pattern. When the mech reached the top of the energy dome that was the Atomic Wave it went into freefall. Steel Samurai 2.0 slammed down into the marsh roughly a quarter mile from where Atomic Rex was standing.

Chris's ears were ringing and his head hurt from being bounced around in his pilot's chair. Alarms were going off throughout the cockpit. He was thankful to see that while the mech had sustained some damage to its external hull that none of its vital systems had been damaged. Chris checked his external feed to see Atomic Rex walking toward him. He attempted to have Steel Samurai 2.0 lift itself off the ground, but he found that when the mech pushed against the soft bottom of the swamp, it only caused it to sink further into the muddy bottom of the marsh.

Chris was fully aware that if Atomic Rex reached him while he was stuck in the mud that he was dead, Steel Samurai 2.0 was going to be destroyed, the people in the Peruvian camp were going to die when Liopleviathan attacked, and that Kate would spend the rest of her life in the clutches of Yetaiju. Chris tried to ignite the mech's rockets to fly out of the mud, but the rockets themselves were also clogged.

There was a deafening roar, and the entire hull of Steel Samurai 2.0 shook as if it was at the epicenter of an earthquake. Chris could hear metal bending and twisting as the cockpit seemed to shift down in front of him. He looked at his external feed to see Atomic Rex pressing his right foot down on Steel Samurai 2.0 as he raised his head in the air and prepared to bite a chunk out of the mech. Tears started to run down Chris's face, but they weren't because of his impending death. He looked at Kate's empty seat next to him and he said, "I am sorry, Kate. I failed you."

Chris took one last look at his visual feed to see Atomic Rex's mouth coming down toward him when suddenly the monster roared in pain and pulled his foot off Steel Samurai 2.0. Chris watched in disbelief as seven long dark brown serpentine heads wrapped themselves around Atomic Rex's legs, arms, torso, and throat. Chris followed the seven heads to a single-wide base, and he let a cheer out as Anacondoid continued to pull Atomic Rex off of his mech.

Atomic Rex turned his back on Steel Samurai 2.0 so he could face this new threat. Chris could see Atomic Rex's tail swinging in front of his robot as the saurian creature struggled to free himself from Anacondoid's grip. Chris quickly grabbed Steel Samurai 2.0's controls, and he used the mech's free hand to reach out and grab the kaiju's tail. The mech pulled hard on the tail, and the kaiju reacted by pulling his tail back toward his body, and in doing so, he also pulled the mech free of the mud it was stuck in. Chris had Steel Samurai 2.0 reach for firmer ground, and when the mech's fingers reached a part of the marsh bed that they didn't sink into, he used it for the mech to grab a handhold and pull itself to a standing position.

Chris had Steel Samurai 2.0 pull each of its legs out of the water and bang them against the other to clear out the mud that had clogged his rockets. He took one last look at Atomic Rex struggling to free himself from Anacondoid's grip then took off into the sky in the direction of Venezuela and Innsmouth.

Atomic Rex could feel his air supply being cut off and his bones being crushed within Anacondoid's grip. The nuclear theropod had the energy within his body to unleash another Atomic Wave, but it would take his cells time to gather the energy after having just unleashed a blast against Steel Samurai 2.0. Atomic Rex tried to roar, but his throat was too constricted for him to do so.

Anacondoid continued to apply pressure to Atomic Rex while simultaneously lifting the saurian creature off the ground. With his legs no longer standing on the ground, Atomic Rex found that he was not able to try and pull away from Anacondoid. Atomic Rex could see that Anacondoid had one of his long necks wrapped around each of his arms and that the serpent was trying to pull his arms as far apart from each other as possible. Atomic Rex began focusing all of his incredible strength and pulling his arms within reach of one another. As Atomic Rex continued to struggle against the pull of the serpent monster, he was slowly pulling his arms closer together. The nuclear theropod's ribs were about to crack when he was finally able to pull his left arm within reach of his right claw. When he finally had a chance to attack Anacondoid, Atomic Rex viciously dug his right claw into the neck wrapped around his left arm.

Blood began to gush out of Anacondoid as Atomic Rex pushed his claw deep into the snakelike neck. When the claw reached Anacondoid's spine and it began to tear into it, the serpentine kaiju was forced to release his grip and pull away from his prey. When Anacondoid released Atomic Rex, the saurian kaiju fell face first into the swamp. The kaiju lifted his head out of the water, and he took two deep breaths before he saw Anacondoid slithering back toward him.

Atomic Rex roared in anger at the creature that had ambushed him. Once more when Anacondoid was near Atomic Rex, the loathsome serpent began his attack by wrapping several of his heads around Atomic Rex's legs. Before the serpent could make his way farther up Atomic Rex's body, the saurian kaiju reached down with his claw and slashed three of the snake monster's necks in half. At the loss of three of its necks, Anacondoid's four remaining heads reared up in front of Atomic Rex. When Atomic Rex saw Anacondoid's remaining four heads in front of him, he lunged forward. Atomic Rex closed his jaws around the middle two heads and he tore them to pieces with a single bite. With each of his claws, he grabbed one of the two remaining outer heads of Anacondoid. Atomic Rex roared at the heads held captive in his claws as he placed his foot on the base of the serpent's body where all of its heads were connected together. Atomic Rex then pulled on the two heads while pushing down with is foot until he managed to tear the heads off what remained of Anacondoid's body.

Atomic Rex roared once more, proclaiming his victory over yet another kaiju. The nuclear theropod then began to devour the remains of his enemy.

CHAPTER 21

SOUTHERN BRAZIL

Kate watched the yeti as he continued to move in a northern direction with a singular determination. She was fully aware that kaiju would often cross great distances in a short amount of time when either patrolling their territory or hunting, but this was something different. Kate had only seen this type of focus and obsessive behavior exhibited by a kaiju in one other instance. When one of the women who was trapped with her attempted to escape Ogre's lair, the monster would pursue them in the same manner that Yetaiju was currently making his way north with her.

While Kate was sure that he was pursuing something, she could not figure out specifically what the kaiju was after. The fact that Yetaiju continued to keep her with him was a clear sign that he felt the need to have humans around him just as Ogre did. From what the beast had displayed so far, she was sure that Yetaiju had enhanced senses of sight, smell, and hearing. Kate was sure that Yetaiju was fully aware that there was a settlement of people in Peru, and yet the monster kept walking in the opposite direction of the campsite.

Kate kept thinking about how Ogre would react when one of his women escaped. Whenever the monster would return from one of his hunts to find that one of his captives had escaped, he would immediately set off to retrieve her. Ogre would not rest until he found the escaped woman and brought her home. He had chased Kate across most of the United States when she escaped from him, and Ogre would still be pursuing her to this day had he not died in battle with Atomic Rex.

Kate kept thinking that if Yetaiju was searching for more humans to surround himself with, then why did he continue to move away from the campsite in Peru? Kate and Chris had scouted South America for years, and she was sure that there was no other settlement in Brazil or the northeastern part of the continent. She thought that if Ogre had wanted to capture more women to keep with him, he would have headed directly for Peru and he would have crushed anything his path.

Kate slowly started to realize that she needed to put away the biases and prejudices that she had acquired from her time with Ogre when thinking of Yetaiju. While there were some similarities between Ogre's actions and Yetaiju's, there were also some differences. Kate knew that if she truly wanted to put an end to the threat posed by Yetaiju, she needed to understand the beast on his own terms rather than through her fears and memories of Ogre.

Kate began to examine the differences between Ogre and Yetaiju. She was doing this not only to help her think more clearly about what was driving Yetaiju's actions but also to help her make a clear delineation between the two monsters in her mind.

While Ogre was always brutal to the women he had captured, Yetaiju seemed to be at least somewhat cognizant of the fact that Kate was fragile. When Ogre moved her or the other woman from place to place, he would handle them as if they were ragdolls and fling them over his shoulder without a care for hurting them. Yetaiju was much larger than Ogre, and he could have easily crushed Kate with the slightest movement of his hand, yet the beast was careful to keep his grip on Kate as loose as possible. In fact, most of the time that he carried Kate, he would hold his hand palm up and keep it open so that Kate could sit in it without him holding on to her.

There was also the very fact that Yetaiju was taking Kate with him as he walked. Whenever Ogre captured a woman, he would immediately take her back to his lair and force her to remain there. Yetaiju did not seem to have a permanent destination. As far as she knew, the yeti had come from Antarctica then entered South America. Since he had first entered South America, he had slain two kaiju whose territories he could have settled in and claimed as his own, yet the beast continued to wander.

Kate decided that she may be better to understand Yetaiju by comparing him to the yeti known as Yukon that her great aunt had encountered in Antarctica. Kate's great aunt had told her how Yukon had captured her friend, Gina, and other women from the nearby tribe in an attempt to rebuild the family that he had lost. Kate considered this information in relation to Yetaiju.

There had been no other yetis sighted besides Yetaiju, so it was likely he was the last of his kind. Based on Yukon's actions, it was reasonable for Kate to assume that Yetaiju would seek to create a surrogate family just as Yukon had, and the fact that he had captured Kate and was keeping her with him supported this hypothesis. Kate's great aunt had also said that Yukon had a cave where he would take the women that he had captured. This behavior was relatable to Ogre in that he would bring women back to his warehouse, but again, it made Yetaiju's current behavior all the more difficult to understand.

If Yetaiju was simply planning to rebuild a family for himself, why was he continuing in a northeastern direction with Kate in his hand? He could have put in some cave in one of the territories he had claimed from the kaiju he had killed; he could have taken her with him to Peru and have captured all of those people then set his home up there. With these options available to him, why would Yetaiju continue to move away from what he perceived as his new potential family, and why would he keep Kate with him?

Suddenly, it was like a tidal wave of insight came crashing down into her mind as she asked these questions about the yeti and realized those questions were perfectly applicable to her as well. Why did she leave her people and her children to venture out into new and dangerous territory? For her, the answer was simple: to protect them from looming threats in the form of Yetaiju and Atomic Rex. She looked up at Yetaiju's human-like face and she could see the same obsession and determination in the yeti's eyes that were in her own. Somewhere in Brazil or farther north, there was something that Yetaiju considered to be a threat to his new family. Whatever this threat was, the yeti felt the need to destroy it before it had the chance to threaten his family. While Kate had thought the best way to keep her family safe was to leave them at the campsite, Yetaiju clearly thought the best way to keep her safe was to take her with him.

Kate began to wonder how Yetaiju could have been aware of such a threat to his new family. She glanced up at the yeti's face again, and she saw something else that she could relate to in his eyes. The pain and anger that only came when someone's entire family was wiped out in front of him. In the years that Kate had lived under Ogre's rule, she had come to view the other women she was trapped with as her family. One by one, she watched as Ogre killed various members of her family for trying to escape. Seeing this not only made Kate hate Ogre, but it also forced her to cut herself off from her need for a family. Even after Chris had rescued her from Ogre, she kept herself distant from him emotionally because she feared that Ogre would hunt down and kill everyone she loved. It wasn't until Chris had shown her that Atomic Rex could potentially kill Ogre that she started to open up to him emotionally. Then, it wasn't until after she saw Ogre die that the prospect of starting a family with Chris began to become a potential reality in her mind.

As Kate looked at Yetaiju, she could see the pain that he was carrying in his mind. It was the pain over a family that he had lost. He had clearly been mutated by a kaiju that had made its way into his valley in Antarctica. It was entirely likely that this kaiju ate a large portion of the animal population in the valley, including Yetaiju's former family. Yetaiju must have obviously survived this attack, mutated, then headed to South America in search of new family. In order to create this new family though, he most likely would have felt the need to avenge the loss of his previous family while also eliminating a threat posed to his new one. Kate understood these motivations because in many ways they were her own. Yetaiju was chasing down his own personal Ogre.

Kate put her face in her hands and she began to cry over what she had realized. There were many similarities between Ogre's behavior and Yetaiju's. The similarities between the two monsters along with Yetaiju's own actions certainly warranted Kate's concern that Yetaiju was a threat to her people and to her children.

Still, Kate was faced with the realization that for as many similarities as there were between Ogre's and Yetaiju's behaviors, there were even more similarities between Yetaiju's actions and her own.

Fifteen miles north of Kate and Yetaiju's current location, a massive creature was awoken from his slumber by the scent of an invader in his territory. The kaiju tilted his head to the side and the large horns that stuck out of the plate which covered his head dug deep into the ground. Styracadon stood, and as he did so the horns on the side of his head tore up several trees that had been caught beneath them. When he was fully standing on two legs the kaiju rotated his shoulders and the two long horns which were protruding from his shoulder blades circled around his back like knives. Styracadon reached out with his claw, and he ran it along the horn on the tip of his snout to sharpen it in preparation for battle. The horned beast slammed his tail into the ground, lifted his head into the air, and roared. As the roar echoed across the sky, Styracadon slowly returned his head to its normal position, and then he began walking directly toward Yetaiju.

Yetaiju heard Styracadon's challenge echo through the jungle. The yeti knew that he was close to reaching Armorsaur. He could also sense that the kaiju which had just challenged him was the last obstacle between himself and his prey. Yetaiju roared in response to Styracadon's challenge then began running toward the monster whose territory he had entered.

Kate pushed her body as flat as she could against Yetaiju's palm while he was running. Thankfully, Yetaiju had partially cupped his hand which was helping to prevent Kate from falling well over one hundred feet to her death. As she bounced in the gargantuan yeti's hand, she held on to her radio as tight as she could. She was fully aware that the radio represented her best hope of surviving and seeing Chris and her children again. Each time that Yetaiju's foot slammed into the ground, Kate's body was thrown into the air and came crashing down against the hard surface of the kaiju's hand. Kate's entire body was being battered and bruised simply by the act of Yetaiju running. When the beast finally came to a stop, Kate moaned in pain and rolled onto her back. She heard an unfamiliar roar, and she rolled over to see Styracadon standing across from Yetaiju.

Yetaiju carefully bent down and placed his hand on the ground. He then tilted his hand so that Kate was able to slide off it and safely onto the ground. Yetaiju continued to watch Kate as she slowly backed away from him, and when she faded into the jungle, the yeti roared and ran toward Styracadon.

When she was in the trees, Kate quickly grabbed her radio and called her husband, "Chris, I only have a minute. We are in southern Brazil. I remain in Yetaiju's possession, but I am still unharmed. He is about to engage Styracadon in battle. What is your current position and progress?"

Chris replied quickly, "We had to take a slight detour from the original plan. Atomic Rex is in Colombia. He has killed Slaughterhouse and El Lobo Blanco. He is currently engaged in a battle with Anacondoid. I am flying into Innsmouth's territory to draw him into a confrontation with the victor. Whichever monster is left standing I will draw out into the Pacific and lead him into a confrontation with Liopleviathan. Then, I am coming for you." Chris was silent for a moment. Then with all of the courage he had, he pleaded with his wife, "Please just tell me that you will still be alive when I come for you. Even if you have to lie to me now, please just tell me that."

A tear ran down Kate's face. "I will be alive when you come for me, Chris. Just stick to your plan. Save the people in Peru and ensure the safety our campsite and our kids, and I promise you I will still be alive when you come for me."

Styracadon charged Yetaiju, and when he was close to the yeti, the horned kaiju lowered his head and aimed his nasal horn at Yetaiju's chest. When Yetaiju saw the horn coming for him, he swung his body to the left so that the horn only grazed his chest rather than plunged into it. Styracadon's momentum carried him forward, and as he was moving past Yetaiju, the primate struck the reptile in his face. Despite hitting his opponent with enough force to shatter a boulder, Yetaiju's blow merely bounced off the thick shield that covered Styracadon's face. Styracadon quickly turned toward Yetaiju, bent down, then brought his head. Yetaiju was able to lean away from the attack, but Styracadon's horn still caught enough of the yeti to cut him from his hip to his shoulder.

Yetaiju quickly ducked under Styracadon's head and wrapped his arms around the horned monster's waist. The yeti then lifted Styracadon off his feet and slammed him to the ground face first. Yetaiju stepped forward to reign down blows on the back his fallen opponent's head, but as he closed on Styracadon, the reptilian beast began to rotate his shoulder blades. Rotating his shoulder blades caused the two long horns protruding from them to spin in tight circles like the blades of a blender. When Yetaiju bent down to strike Styracadon, his forearm received a deep cut from the rotating horns which caused the yeti to back away from the horned monster.

As Yetaiju ceased his attack, Styracadon regained his feet, roared, and charged at Yetaiju. Yetaiju once again side-stepped the attack, but this time when Styracadon missed his charge, the reptilian kaiju spun away from the yeti and drug the horns on his back across the primate's chest. Yetaiju backed away from his opponent as blood dripped down his body from multiple cuts on his arms and torso. Yetaiju roared at his opponent then leapt at Styracadon once more, ducking under the kaiju's head and out of the range of his horns. Yetaiju wrapped his arms around Styracadon's chest, and then he grabbed the monster's back horns with his claws and began freezing them with the icy mist from his hands.

Styracadon struggled to break free from the icy grip, but the yeti's strength was too powerful for him to overcome. Yetaiju continued to apply his freezing to Styracadon's back horns until he felt them become brittle and shatter. With the back horns shattered, Yetaiju again lifted Styracadon off his feet then slammed him face first into the ground. Styracadon was trying to stand when Yetaiju jumped on his back and forced the horned monster back to the ground. Yetaiju sat on Styracadon's shoulders then placed his hands under the kaiju's jaw. Yetaiju pulled back on Styracadon's jaw, forcing his head to bend backward until the kaiju's neck finally broke. Yetaiju growled as he wrenched Styracadon's head off its body. He then lifted the decapitated head into the air and roared. After he had unleashed his roar, he tossed Styracadon's head into the jungle and he took the time to devour a few bites of Styracadon's body. When Yetaiju was finished eating he walked over to the area where he had put down Kate.

Kate was on her radio updating Chris on her location and the events that had occurred. "Yetaiju has just killed Styracadon. He is coming for me. I love you, and I will update you again when I have the chance."

She looked up to see to see the blood-soaked Yetaiju towering above her. The beast reached down and carefully scooped up Kate. With Kate in his grasp once again, Yetaiju continued his trek north in search of Armorsaur.

Yetaiju walked for over two hours and covered nearly one hundred miles before he finally decided to rest. The yeti carefully placed Kate on the ground, then remembering what Beach Master had done to the other walruses that surrounded him, Yetaiju carefully backed away from Kate before lying down to avoid accidentally crushing her.

Kate found a tree to prop herself up against and she walked over to it, leaned her back against the trunk of the ancient tree, and slid to the ground. She was sitting with her back against the tree and her head between her knees. She heard Yetaiju moving, and she looked up to see that the yeti had rolled to his side and was staring at her.

At first, she was reminded of the way that Ogre used to stare at her, but this was a different stare from Ogre's. Ogre used to watch over her with the intensity of a prison guard. He was always waiting for Kate or one of the other women to try and escape so that he could either chase them down or punish them.

The look the Yetaiju was giving her was different from that. Kate thought that Yetaiju was staring at her as if he was resigning himself to a new life. She began to imagine the yeti thinking about the family he had lost and then looking at her as the sorry excuse for the next best option. It was that feeling, the feeling of knowing that the yeti would never be able to fill the void in his life, that made Kate fear the creature instead of pity him.

Kate had initially compared Yetaiju to Ogre, but she was wrong. Yetaiju was far more dangerous than Ogre. Kate had been around Ogre long enough to know that the brute was not very intelligent. Ogre had some vague sense that he should surround himself with others. He didn't need to feel as if the people he had around him cared for him. Ogre simply felt that having people around was enough to make him feel like he was part of something. In his twisted mind, Ogre felt like he was in a group that he belonged in and that was why keeping a handful of women around him was enough to keep him happy.

Kate could see that simply having people around him would not be enough to satisfy Yetaiju. She knew that Yetaiju would never be able to find the sense of belonging or companionship that he needed, and because of that, he would continue to search for it. This sense of emptiness would drive him to try and fill it, and Kate wouldn't be enough. Yetaiju would keep kidnapping people and trying to find someone that made him feel as if he was part of a family. Yetaiju would take the people in the campsite in Peru, he would take the people from her campsite, the monster would eventually take her children. Kate feared that the eventual outcome would be worse than being trapped by Ogre. She feared that if Yetaiju was unable to find what he wanted in the people he took, he would take his anger out on them.

Kate watched as the massive yeti slowly drifted off to sleep. When she was sure that Yetaiju would not wake up, she used her portable radio to send a message in Morse code to Emily and Kyle.

She was surprised when Emily's voice came back on the radio, "Mom, you're alive. You don't need to use Morse code anymore, we can talk freely."

Kate was surprised at her daughter's response. "Isn't the council still trying to block communications between the two of us?"

Emily laughed. "No, they have decided to step down. They are helping hold things together until you get back, but once we get everyone back from the evacuation, they have decided to hold free elections for their positions."

Kate was stunned at the events that had unraveled in the short time that she was gone. "Evacuation? Start at the beginning and fill me everything."

Emily collected her thoughts and filled her mother in on the events that had occurred at their campsite. "First, when Atomic Rex crossed the Rockies, we had to lure him into Behemoth's territory. Atomic Rex killed Behemoth, and then Dad picked him up from there. Atomic Rex scared Ramrod who went on a rampage up the coast. We had to evacuate everyone before Ramrod got here. Kyle and I devised a plan to set a forest fire and scare off Ramrod, but we had also prepared the town for the evacuation and had started it as soon as we heard about Ramrod. I went to the council leader and told him that he wasn't much of leader but that these people needed him to lead the evacuation while we took care Ramrod. I also told him that I would hold him responsible if he failed the people or tried to do something stupid to undermine you. It seems that over the course of the evacuation, a lot of the people we had pre-warned to get ready to leave were calling the council elder out on it and said that he had nearly cost them their lives. People started saying that simply being there a long time didn't qualify the council as leaders and that the council should be elected just like you were. When Kyle and I returned to the campsite and called the evacuees back home, the council leader came off the boat, told us about what the townspeople had said, agreed they were right, and said he would step down as soon you got home."

Kate was dumbfounded. In a matter of a few days, her children had diverted two kaiju attacks, evacuated the town, and had inadvertently dethroned the council that she had struggled with for fifteen years. What was more astounding was the fact that Emily had done all of this as if it was a part of everyday life. Kate shook her head and smiled as she replied to her daughter, "Emily, you are amazing."

Emily giggled. "I know. My boyfriend hasn't stopped saying that since we got back from diverting Ramrod."

With all of the information that Kate had received from her daughter, this was the news that she was most excited about. "Your boyfriend? Okay, now start from when I left and tell me everything."

Despite being on separate continents and being surrounded by monsters, Kate and Emily talked as mother and daughter. Their conversation of Emily's first boyfriend helped them to laugh, feel excited, and give them some comfort that despite all that had gone on, they were still a family. After talking to Emily for an hour about Sean, Kate said good night to her daughter and she said that she would be home soon. Before drifting off to sleep, Kate glared at the sleeping Yetaiju. "There is no way that I am letting you live long enough to try and take her."

She laughed once before going to sleep as she thought to herself that they needed to keep from Chris that Emily had a boyfriend.

She knew that even with his wife in the clutches of a monster, and the fate of the human race resting on his shoulders, that if he found out Emily had a boyfriend, the first thing he would do is land Steel Samurai 2.0 in front of Sean and put the fear of God in him.

CHAPTER 22

VENEZUELA ANGEL FALLS

Chris looked down at an odd juxtaposition of both beauty and horror as he flew over his target. Below him was Angel Falls, the tallest waterfall in the world with a height of over three thousand feet at its apex. While the falls were one of nature's wonders, the creature that had taken up residency in the water at the base of the falls was truly an abomination.

Chris had battled a multitude of kaiju over his life, but none of them unnerved him as much as Innsmouth did. Chris looked down to see the creature swimming in a circle in the water at the base of the falls. Chris could see its large shark-like fin sticking out of the water as it swam. He could also see the rest of the monster's huge body through the water. What most disturbed Chris about Innsmouth was that his body had a humanoid form to it. The kaiju looked like a giant man cover in fish scales with the head of a piranha and a shark's fin on top of it. The creature also had large claws on its hands and feet and a thin sail running down its back, but for the most part, the creature looked like some kind of eerie cross between a man and a fish. Kate had told Chris that the monster's name came from a story where a town of people had turned themselves into fish people to appease some ancient god.

Chris knew that Innsmouth was reported to be a larger version of a species of fish man that had come from the same island as Atomic Rex and the other true kaiju. The theory was that the species was some form of alternative branch of fish that had adapted to living part of their lives on land. Chris had always thought the writer who created the idea of people making a deal with some ancient god or devil was a much more fitting explanation for Innsmouth because he had a hard time believing that nature could create such a horrid species of animal.

Whatever the explanation for Innsmouth's existence was, all that Chris knew was that he hated the creature and he would be glad when its existence was ended. Chris circled Steel Samurai 2.0 around the sky above the falls twice then dove straight at the horrific creature.

Steel Samurai 2.0 slammed into Innsmouth and smashed the kaiju's head into the riverbed. Innsmouth quickly turned around and raked his claws across the mech's chest, gouging through the outer layer of its hull. Chris quickly sealed off the areas of the hull where water was entering into Steel Samurai 2.0, and then he turned on the mech's interior pumps to dispose of any water that had made its way into the mech.

Chris had the mech deliver two quick punches to the monster's face that made Innsmouth swim away from him. When the kaiju retreated, Chris had the robot assume a standing position. As Steel Samurai 2.0 rose to his full height, Innsmouth stopped swimming away from him and he stood as well. Both the mech and the kaiju were staring at each other in waist deep water.

Innsmouth hissed at Steel Samurai 2.0, which indicated to Chris that he had sufficiently angered the kaiju to the point that he would follow him. Steel Samurai 2.0 flew up through the cascading water to the top of the waterfall. Chris was hovering above the top of the waterfall, and he looked down to see Innsmouth's climbing up the waterfall as easily as a monkey would scale a tree. Chris backed the mech away from the edge of the waterfall, and then he began flying over the river and back in the direction of Colombia. Behind him, Innsmouth was swimming through the river with the speed of living torpedo as he chased Steel Samurai 2.0. Chris did some quick calculations, and he guessed that at the speed they were moving they would reach the edge of Anacondoid's territory in slightly over an hour. From there, it was just a matter of finding either the snake monster or Atomic Rex.

Chris's mind was racing and he was pushing himself as hard as he could. His wife was in the possession of a giant yeti, and he still needed to contrive three more kaiju battles and fly across a continent twice before he would have the chance to try and rescue her. He whispered to himself, "Please be alive, Kate."

50 miles off the coast of Peru

The sun was shining down and the wind was blowing in from the west as a giant mutant seagull sat on the surface of the ocean. The bird bobbed up and down with the waves as they rolled beneath her. The creature had a wingspan that was over one hundred feet long, and she had a beak that was strong enough to shatter concrete. She was sitting as still as she could on the water as she searched for large fish that she could snatch out of the sea. The giant gull's keen eyes were scanning the water below it when she suddenly saw a huge dark shape coming up from the depths below her. The bird immediately began to flap her wings and take to the sky. She has risen roughly fifty feet off the surface of the ocean when Liopleviathan burst out of the water beneath her. The sea monster's jaws reached out and closed on the giant bird just below its neck. The seagull was able to let a brief screech before Liopleviathan pulled the doomed mutant back below the waves. Liopleviathan chomped down twice on his prey before continuing on his path toward the shores of South America.

Colombia

Atomic Rex had finished devouring the remains of the fallen Anacondoid, and he started moving east in the direction that he had seen Steel Samurai 2.0 fly off in. He had entered the Meta River and was making his way up it when he saw the hated mech flying over the water and coming directly toward him. The kaiju's eyes went wide when he saw his enemy. The monster roared a challenge at the robot, but to the Atomic Rex's surprise, the mech flew right over him without engaging him in battle. Atomic Rex was standing in water up to his hips as he turned around and looked at Steel Samurai 2.0 hovering in the river behind him. The kaiju was about to attack the mech when another scent caught his attention.

Atomic Rex quickly turned around to see a large swell of water moving quickly through the river toward him. The swell came to a stop, and Innsmouth lifted the upper half of his body out of the river. The fish man hissed at the creature before he and Atomic Rex responded with a roar that sent ripples rolling across the surface of the river.

Innsmouth dove into the water and swam at Atomic Rex with a speed the nuclear theropod was unprepared for. Innsmouth wrapped his arms around Atomic Rex's right thigh, and then he stood with the leg still in his grasp, causing Atomic Rex to tumble backward into the river. The aquatic horror pounced on Atomic Rex, using his claws and teeth to tear into the saurian kaiju's face.

A cloud of blood quickly formed around Atomic Rex's head, obscuring his vision of his attacker. One of Innsmouth's claws slashed across Atomic Rex's chest, missing his neck by only a few feet. Atomic Rex quickly brought his feet up underneath him and placed them on Innsmouth's midsection. Atomic Rex then extended his legs and pushed Innsmouth off his chest.

Both monsters rose out of the water and stared at each other. Atomic Rex began moving toward Innsmouth, and the two kaiju started exchanging blows in the middle of the river. Chris saw a blur of punches, claw gouges, forearm strikes, and head butts as the two monsters fought. It was easy for Chris to see that it was Atomic Rex who was getting the better of the exchange, as with each blow he was forcing Innsmouth to give ground. When his opponent was off balance, Atomic Rex stepped forward, pushed Innsmouth backward, and sent the fish man tumbling into the river.

As soon as he splashed down into the river, Innsmouth shifted his body around. He remained under water as he swam past Atomic Rex and then behind him. Innsmouth exploded out of the water behind Atomic Rex, and then he jumped on the nuclear theropod's back. Innsmouth sank his piranha-like fangs into Atomic Rex's shoulder then bit a large chunk out of it. The giant fish man then ran his claws down Atomic Rex's back, carving several large gashes into it.

Atomic Rex roared in pain as Innsmouth continued to rip his back apart. Atomic Rex reached over his shoulder and grabbed Innsmouth by the head. He then lowered his shoulder and pulled forward, flipping Innsmouth off his back and throwing the fish man into the river in front of him.

Innsmouth popped out of the water with his claws raised above his head and ready to strike. Before Innsmouth had the chance to lower his hands, Atomic Rex stepped forward with his head lowered and delivered a head butt to Innsmouth's face. The blow caused Innsmouth to stumble backward. Atomic Rex followed up the head butt with alternating strikes from his claws to Innsmouth's face, further staggering the creature. Innsmouth was losing his balance as Atomic Rex was moving in for the kill. In an act of desperation, Innsmouth slashed at Atomic Rex with his right claw. Atomic Rex's forward motion allowed Innsmouth's claw to cut deep into his neck. The nuclear theropod's neck had blood pouring out of it, but despite the mortal wound, the kaiju continued moving forward until he was able to close his jaws on Innsmouth's head. Atomic Rex crushed Innsmouth's head while using his claws to slice open his opponent's chest.

Atomic Rex's continued to bleed profusely from his neck as his shook his opponent until he died. When Innsmouth finally expired, Atomic Rex released the monster then walked over to the riverbank and collapsed.

Chris flew Steel Samurai 2.0 closer to the injured monster. He zoomed his cameras in on the injured kaiju's neck. He could see the wound closing relatively quickly, but he could also see that Atomic Rex was exhausted. Chris had always thought that the monster's stamina and endurance were limitless, but then he considered the amount of battles that the kaiju had engaged in over a span of only two days.

Chris looked down at the resting monster, and he thought to himself that this was the chance he had dreamed of for fifteen years. Atomic Rex was exhausted and injured before him while Steel Samurai 2.0 was functioning at nearly one hundred percent. He knew that all he had to do was to use Steel Samurai's sword to cut the monster's head off and end its life once and for all.

At the same time, he knew that he needed Atomic Rex alive and at full power to fight Yetaiju so that he had the chance to save Kate. Chris was faced with the decision of ending the life of the object of his hatred for the past fifteen years at the expense of placing the love of his life and potentially the lives of his children and friends in danger as well if Yetaiju lived.

He sighed as looked down at Atomic Rex and made a promise to his lifelong enemy, "I know that I am going to regret this, but I swear to you, one day I will finally kill you."

Chris had Steel Samurai 2.0 land and move close to Atomic Rex. He then had the robot open its chest and expose the nuclear reactor that powered it. Chris could actually see the radiation being given off from the reactor flowing down onto the body of Atomic Rex as the monster drew the energy into him. Atomic Rex began to stir and the wounds on him that were still in the process of healing themselves immediately closed and grew new scales over them.

Atomic Rex's eyes snapped open, and when he saw Steel Samurai 2.0 standing above him, the monster sprang to his feet! Chris quickly had the mech punch the kaiju in the face and the pilot sneered. "You're welcome!" He then had Steel Samurai 2.0 fly into the air where he had the mech close its chest and stop the flow of radiation to the kaiju.

Atomic Rex was roaring at Steel Samurai, and Chris was confident that the monster was fully recharged and ready for battle. He had no sooner finished that thought than a call came over the ham radio system, "Attention Captain Myers, this is General Mendoza. Liopleviathan has been spotted off our coast. We will soon experience flooding and then the creature may try to come ashore. We are in desperate need of your help. Please reply."

Chris grabbed his radio. "This is Captain Myers. I copy and I am on my way! Over!" Chris then turned Steel Samurai 2.0 in the direction of Peru and he took off at Mach 5.

Atomic Rex roared at the fleeing mech, and then he began sprinting in the direction the robot had flown off in.

CHAPTER 23

NORTHERN BRAZIL

Kate was sound asleep with her back still against the tree when Yetaiju suddenly sat up and started grunting. Kate quickly woke up to see the giant yeti still sitting in the same spot where he had slept, but the beast was now fully awake and alert. Yetaiju was looking in a northern direction and sniffing the air. After sniffing the air several times, the kaiju's body went rigid. Yetaiju didn't move for several seconds, but then Kate could see the yeti's facial expression slowly starting to change. Yetaiju's brow furled and he pulled his lips back to reveal his teeth. Then Kate looked at Yetaiju's eyes, and she saw an anger in them that she had only experienced one other time in her life. The look of anger in Yetaiju's eyes was the same look that she had right before she jammed a blowtorch into Ogre's teeth as he was tearing a hole in the original Steel Samurai. The look in the yeti's eyes was the look of someone who had been seeking vengeance for a horrible deed that had been done to someone they loved.

Yetaiju stood up and he roared at the jungle to the north with the fury of an erupting volcano. Kate heard a rumbling and the sound of trees being knocked over. She heard something large slam into the ground then the sound of a roar in reply. At the sound of the roar, Yetaiju went into a fury. He bent down and began pounding his fists into the ground. He then ripped up every tree within his reach and tossed them into the air.

Kate looked to the north, and she could see trees being knocked down by some large creature, but whatever the creature was, it was only slightly taller than the tree canopy. As the monster came a few steps closer, she could see countless sharp spikes jutting out of every direction attached to a hard caprice. Kate gasped when she saw a long scorpion-like tail swinging above the tree canopy. She knew then what kaiju was coming for them. A flat brown head that ended in a bony knob and long sharp claws similar to those of an armadillo poked out of the trees to reveal Armorsaur.

The kaiju was built like a living tank. His armor made him nearly invulnerable, and his scorpion-like tail was far more destructive than the firepower of any tank mankind had ever constructed. Yetaiju unleashed not a roar but a howl that made Kate's entire body shiver. Kate had heard Yetaiju roar in anger, but this was a howl filled with anguish. The howl confirmed Kate's suspicions about how Yetaiju had come into being. The monster was indeed a mutated yeti whose family had been killed by a kaiju prior to his mutating. As Yetaiju sprinted toward Armorsaur, it was clear that the spiked kaiju was the monster that had killed his family.

When Kate saw Yetaiju battle Styracadon, she was amazed at the monster's intelligence. Yetaiju looked for weaknesses to exploit while at the same time identifying Styracadon's strengths then trying to avoid them. Yetaiju defeated Styracadon by outthinking him more than overpowering him. Conversely, Yetaiju's attack on Armorsaur was nothing but pure rage. Yetaiju ran up to Armorsaur and immediately began pounding on the reptilian monster's spiked back. Blood spurted from Yetaiju's fists as Armorsaur ignored the ineffectual blows and lifted his tail in the air behind him. Yetaiju was still pounding on Armorsaur's spikes when the four-legged kaiju drove his stinger into the yeti's shoulder.

Yetaiju roared in pain as Armorsaur twisted his stinger from side to side, driving it deeper into the yeti's shoulder. Yetaiju grabbed the stinger with both of his hands, and he was trying to pull it out of his shoulder when Armorsaur stepped forward and drove the knob on his head into Yetaiju's knee. The blow buckled the yeti's knee and caused him to fall to the ground. Yetaiju suddenly found himself kneeling in front of Armorsaur with the reptilian monster's tail still embedded in his shoulder. Armorsaur charged forward and drove the protruding bone on top of his head into Yetaiju's nose. Kate heard a loud crack then she saw watched as Yetaiju fell flat on his back with his face totally covered in blood.

Kate was shocked at the way that the battle was unfolding before her. Yetaiju had the speed, agility, and intelligence to make short work of Armorsaur, but he had let his emotions overwhelm him, and now he was going to pay for that mistake with his life. Kate didn't feel any sympathy toward Yetaiju; she had hoped the kaiju would die before he came close to either her campsite or the one in Peru. She had planned, though, for him to die fighting a kaiju Chris had drawn to him so that he was on the spot where she had a chance to enter Steel Samurai 2.0. Now, she was faced with a situation where Armorsaur was about to kill Yetaiju then, in all likelihood, come after her with Chris still on the other side of the continent. She realized that she needed to put as much distance between herself and Armorsaur as possible. She turned away from the fight and she began running into the jungle.

Armorsaur's head moved as Kate ran away. The kaiju knew that the human was an easy meal, and he also knew that the invader to his territory was defeated and dying. Armorsaur pulled his stinger out of Yetaiju's shoulder then took a few steps away from the injured yeti. Armorsaur looked at Yetaiju then lifted his tail in the air behind him. Yetaiju could see the electric charge building at the end of Armorsaur's stinger. Yetaiju started to roll his body away from Armorsaur, but he reacted far too late. A bolt of electrical energy streaked out of Armorsaur's stinger and struck Yetaiju. The yeti's body was racked with pain as millions of volts of electricity were sent running through him. When Armorsaur cut off his blast, Yetaiju's body was still twitching from the shock it had sustained. Armorsaur roared at the defeated yeti, and then he turned and started to chase Kate.

Yetaiju was in horrible physical pain and in mental torment at the same time. The creature who had killed his family and whom he had hunted for days was killing him. He was going to die and the beast that had eaten his family would soon devour him as well. His head lolled to the side just in time to see Kate sprinting into the jungle. The yeti moaned as he realized the creature that was to be a part of his new family was leaving him as well. Yetaiju rolled over onto his stomach and he watched as Armorsaur plodded off after Kate.

When he saw Armorsaur going after the new member of his family, the yeti was again overcome with anger. The kaiju that had killed his previous family was now trying to kill the only creature on this planet that Yetaiju felt any connection to. Adrenaline coursed through Yetaiju's body and renewed his strength. Yetaiju stood and grabbed Armorsaur's tail as the kaiju was walking away. Yetaiju then wrapped his hands around Armorsaur's stinger and he began unleashing his freezing power on it. When the end of Armorsaur's tail was frozen solid, Yetaiju ripped it off the kaiju and threw it at his head.

Yetaiju then slid his hands down to what remained of Armorsaur's tail. The yeti pulled on the tail with enough force to life Armorsaur off the ground and swung his entire body away from Kate. When Yetaiju had swung Armorsaur a full one hundred and eighty degrees away from Kate, he released the monster's tail. The momentum of Armorsaur's body sent the reptilian beast rolling through the jungle. The monster had completely rolled over four times before he was able to stop himself and plant his feet beneath him.

As soon as Armorsaur had stopped rolling, Yetaiju was in front of him. Armorsaur thrust his stingerless tail at Yetaiju, and the yeti simply swiped the ineffectual weapon aside. Armorsaur then lowered his head and charged at Yetaiju, but the nimble yeti was easily able to avoid the slower creature's attack. Yetaiju then grabbed the knob on Armorsaur's head, and the yeti began turning it toward the ground, forcing the reptilian kaiju to roll with it or have his neck broken. Yetaiju continued turning the knob until he managed to flip Armorsaur on his back.

Armorsaur's legs were flailing helplessly in the air as he tried to build enough momentum to flip himself back onto his feet, but Yetaiju had no intention of giving his nemesis that opportunity. Yetaiju ran over to Armorsaur, grabbed his left hind leg in his hands, and then snapped the limb in half. Armorsaur roared in pain at the broken limb while Yetaiju jumped over to his right hind leg and repeated the process, this time causing a compound fracture to occur.

Blood gushed around the bone that protruded from Armorsaur's leg as Yetaiju moved on to Armorsaur's front legs. After he had broken all four of Armorsaur's legs, Yetaiju stood above the monster and he glared down at him. Yetaiju roared at the thought of finally killing the monster that had exterminated his entire species. The giant yeti jumped into the air and brought all of his weight crashing down into Armorsaur's rib cage, breaking several ribs. Yetaiju then howled once more as the images of Armorsaur eating his family ran through his mind. The yeti lifted his hands into the air and he brought them crashing down into Armorsaur's chest. He repeated the move over and over again as the images of each and every one of his sons, mates, and brothers that the monster had eaten flashed through his mind.

When Yetaiju had finally expended his rage, all that remained of Armorsaur was a pool of blood and bones that were floating in a shell which had been driven into the ground. The exhausted yeti lifted himself up out of the remains of his enemy and he sniffed the air. He was immediately able to identify Kate's scent and he started walking after her.

Kate was still running at full speed when she again heard trees crashing down behind her. She knew that Armorsaur was chasing her but she thought that the monster may have momentarily stopped his pursuit because she heard Yetaiju howl. She thought that perhaps Armorsaur had gone back and ended the yeti and was now after her once more.

She strained to push her legs harder, and her mind was racing as he looked for anything that she could possibly hide in that could shield her from the kaiju. Kate felt the ground shake beneath her feet, and in her heart, she knew that she was going to die. She tried to focus on Chris and her kids so that they would be the last thought on her mind as she perished. A shock ran through her body as she felt something huge wrap around it. She braced for the pain of having Armorsaur's teeth crush her body but she instead found herself in the blood-soaked hand of Yetaiju.

The yeti carefully picked her up and brought her to his eye level. He stared long and hard at her as he considered the fact that he had slain the creature that had killed his previous family. With the monster dead, Yetaiju felt as if he could now focus on building a new family with the woman he held in his hand as the first member of it. He sniffed the air, and with his enhanced sense of smell, he was able to detect more yeti-like creatures far away and near another ocean.

Yetaiju longed to set off in pursuit of these new family members, but with the adrenaline rush wearing off his badly injured body, he was in need of rest. Satisfied for the moment that he had reacquired the woman, Yetaiju sat down and placed Kate at arm's length away from him. The battered yeti then laid down and fell asleep.

With Yetaiju sleeping in front of her, Kate quickly turned on her portable radio and called Chris. "Chris, come in. This is Kate. Yetaiju has now killed Armorsaur in northern Brazil. He was heading west when he stopped and fell asleep. Where are you and Atomic Rex currently?"

Chris spoke quickly as he replied, "Atomic Rex killed Innsmouth in Colombia. The last I saw him he was pursuing me. I am currently flying over the flooded section of what was once the Peruvian settlement. Liopleviathan is currently offshore and heading inland." Chris was silent for a moment. "My God, Kate, I can see it more than a half a mile off shore. The creature has to be the largest thing that has ever inhabited this planet."

CHAPTER 24

PERU

Chris watched through his internal feed as hundreds of people ran into the jungle to escape the surge of seawater which heralded Liopleviathan's coming. Chris shook his head in disgust at himself. He was supposed to have cleared a path for these people and to have had them on their way into Central America by the time that Liopleviathan made his way back to Peru. Now here they were, faced with Liopleviathan to the west, Atomic Rex to the north, and Yetaiju to the east.

It was obvious that despite the plans they had made, the group needed to head south for the time being. While there would be giant mutants in the area, at least there were no True Kaiju since Yetaiju had killed them all. Chris grabbed his radio and he tried to contact the camp leader, "General Mendoza, this is Captain Myers. Atomic Rex is inbound from the north and our last report of Yetaiju had him heading this way from the east. You need to move your people in a southern direction. Do you copy?"

Chris waited, but he didn't receive a reply. He knew that he needed to get people moving in a southern direction as quickly as possible, and then he needed to head out over the ocean where he could engage Liopleviathan before the monster came any closer to shore. Chris quickly piloted Steel Samurai 2.0 to the front of the mass of fleeing people. He quickly fired several rounds in the air to make sure he had everyone's attention just in case they were too scared to see the giant mech flying above them. When he could see that the majority of the crowd was looking at him, he had Steel Samurai 2.0 point to the south. The people at the front of the group seemed to understand and they started running in that direction. With the people of Peru no longer heading directly toward Yetaiju, Chris flew his mech toward the largest kaiju in history.

Steel Samurai 2.0 was flying over the ocean when Kate tried to call him. He quickly informed her of what he was looking at then he ended the transmission. He was so in awe of the size of Liopleviathan that for the first time in fifteen years, he forgot to tell his wife that he loved her before ending a communication.

The monster's size was overwhelming. Chris remembered a story from his childhood about a monster known as the Kraken that was so large, sailors would land on its back, thinking that it was an island when it was asleep. He could almost see a ship full of Vikings making that same mistake with Liopleviathan.

The monster was moving just below the surface of the water which complicated things for Chris. He would have preferred to have stayed in the air and engaged the sea monster from there, but he knew that most his weapons would lose effectiveness and accuracy if he tried to fire them from the air through the water. He had several torpedoes designed specifically for engaging targets underwater, but in order to utilize them, Steel Samurai 2.0 would have to be underwater as well. Chris thought that the upgrades he and the engineering team had done to the mech would give Steel Samurai 2.0 an advantage in both speed and agility underwater over Liopleviathan, but the pilot was not overly anxious to test that idea.

Chris knew that he did not have time to debate the issue internally because Liopleviathan was quickly swimming toward land and toward the people who were trying to evacuate the Peruvian campsite. Chris shrugged then had Steel Samurai 2.0 dive into the water roughly a quarter mile in front of the oncoming kaiju. He then used the mech's targeting system to lock his torpedoes on the monster. With the target locked, Chris fired four torpedoes at the oncoming beast. He watched through external feed as the projectiles shot through the water toward the kaiju. Chris shook his head in disbelief when explosion's large enough to have blown a nuclear submarine in half looked like little more than matchsticks as they detonated against the monster.

Liopleviathan ignored the blasts and continued swimming toward Steel Samurai 2.0. Chris quickly fired one more volley of torpedoes at the monster to make sure that the beast's attention was on Steel Samurai 2.0 rather than on the coast. Once again, the explosions did nothing to dissuade the kaiju. Chris hoped that he had done enough to goad the monster into following the mech. He shifted Steel Samurai 2.0 slightly to the left and he began moving parallel to the coastline.

Chris was hit by mixed feelings of relief and anxiety when Liopleviathan altered his course and began pursuing Steel Samurai 2.0. The monster was quickly gaining on the mech, and Chris quickly accelerated the robot to its top speed in the water. When Steel Samurai 2.0 hit its top speed, the mech was moving faster than any man-made creation in the history of the world. Before the end of the world, this feat would have qualified Chris as a hero and put him the company of legends such as Chuck Yeager and John Glenn. As things stood today, he hoped the mech's new speed record would simply be sufficient enough to keep him alive. Chris took a quick look at his sonar screen to see that despite how fast he was going, Liopleviathan was still gaining on him.

At the monster's current speed, Chris surmised that he had roughly one minute before Liopleviathan was closing his jaws around Steel Samurai 2.0. Chris pulled back hard on the controls causing the mech to start rising toward the surface. Steel Samurai 2.0 exploded out of the water and started climbing into the sky just as Liopleviathan breached the surface and threw himself after the robot. The kaiju's massive jaws snapped shut just below Steel Samurai 2.0's feet, giving the monster nothing more than a taste of the mech's exhaust fumes.

After breaching, Liopleviathan continued to swim on the surface of the water as he turned back toward shore. The kaiju was less than a quarter mile from shore, but now his body was exposed above the water. Chris quickly aimed all his weapons at the monster's exposed back. Steel Samurai 2.0 fired enough bullets, missiles, and napalm at Liopleviathan's back to raze a small city to the ground. Once again, to Chris's astonishment, the monster seemed totally unfazed by the attack. Chris shook his head in disbelief. In a matter of less than thirty seconds, he had unloaded every piece of ammunition at his disposal on Liopleviathan, and he had barely managed to slow the creature down.

The beast was now shallow enough that his flippers were touching the bottom of the ocean. Chris was pleased that if nothing else, this had at least slowed the monster down considerably as he was forced to move his huge bulk without the benefit of being able to swim. The monster's back and head were out of the water. Chris knew that he still had to slow the monster down if wanted to make sure that the evacuees had enough time to clear the area before the monster came ashore. Chris looked down at Liopleviathan's huge eye and he said to himself, "If there is any part of you that is vulnerable, that will be it."

Chris then had Steel Samurai 2.0 unsheathe its sword. The mech held the blade out in front of it then it flew directly at Liopleviathan's right eye. The sword punctured the colossal eye like a pin going through a water balloon. Blood and ichor from the injured organ spewed over Steel Samurai 2.0. Liopleviathan then quickly turned his to his right, causing the mech to swing toward him. The kaiju snapped his jaws shut around the mech's left arm, shoulder, and thigh. Chris heard the sound of metal being crushed, as in a single bite, Liopleviathan shredded thirty percent of Steel Samurai 2.0 to scrap.

Chris quickly had the mech take off as high as it was able to in order for him to assess the damage. Alarms were going off through the mech, and Chris quickly sealed off as many damaged sections as he could. Despite the damage to the mech, since the rockets on its feet and back were still intact, the mech was capable of flight but not much else. Chris would be able to use Steel Samurai 2.0 as a transport vehicle, but the mech was no longer able to battle with kaiju in any manner.

Chris hovered above Liopleviathan as the mammoth kaiju continued to make his way toward shore. There was nothing Chris could do to impede the beast. At this point, he was little more than a spectator to the destruction that the monster would wreak on the campsite and its people. Chris's shifted his gaze toward the campsite. Thanks to the Peruvians putting their huts on stilts, most of the huts were surviving the floodwater, but Chris knew that nothing would survive once Liopleviathan reached land. Chris looked at the monster to see that he was less than a hundred yards away from where the huts were. While the super kaiju was moving slower than he did in the water the sheer length of each of his strides was allowing Liopleviathan to cover large amounts of ground in a short time. Chris guessed that if the kaiju went after the fleeing Peruvians, he would catch them in less than half an hour. Chris's mind was racing as he tried to think of some way to slow down the monster or to speed up the evacuees when a familiar roar echoed across the sky.

Chris and Liopleviathan both looked to the jungle beyond the huts to see Atomic Rex making his way toward the beach. Liopleviathan unleashed a roar that was much deeper and louder than Atomic Rex's call as a challenge to the nuclear theropod. Atomic Rex sprinted toward the ocean, eager to slay this new beast and once more prove his supremacy over all that he surveyed.

Chris watched as the two kaiju were walking toward each other. He had suggested that with the help of Steel Samurai 2.0, Atomic Rex would be capable of slaying Liopleviathan. Now as he saw the two monster's approaching each other, he realized how wrong he was. Liopleviathan's jaws alone were larger than Atomic Rex's entire body. Chris began talking to himself, "The thing is going to swallow Atomic Rex whole. There has to be something I can do to help those people. Maybe if I can just grab a few of them at a time, I can fly them farther inland out of Liopleviathan's range."

He looked down to see that Atomic Rex and Liopleviathan had almost reached each other. Even at one hundred and fifty feet tall Atomic Rex's head barely reached Liopleviathan's lower jaw. Liopleviathan towered over Atomic Rex. Chris thought that it was almost as if Liopleviathan was so large that he was kaiju to the kaiju. Chris was certain that Atomic Rex was just about to meet his end when he saw the kaiju's scales take on a bright blue hue. Liopleviathan's jaws shot forward and engulfed Atomic Rex. Then, a split second later, the giant sea monster's entire head exploded as the nuclear theropod unleashed his Atomic Wave prior to Liopleviathan fully closing his jaws. Chris watched in awe as pieces of Liopleviathan's jaw, skull, and brains rained down on the roaring Atomic Rex.

The kaiju shook the remains of the sea monster off his body, and then he looked to the sky at the badly damaged Steel Samurai 2.0 and roared at the hated mech. Chris nodded at the monster and said, "I need you to do one more thing. Then you can either die or live out the rest of your wretched life here. I don't care either way at this point. Just help me get Kate back and then you never have to see me again."

Chris slowly flew Steel Samurai 2.0 over Atomic Rex's head then he set a course for Brazil. He turned on his radio, "Kate, Atomic Rex has killed Liopleviathan. The people of the Peruvian campsite have evacuated to the south for now." He paused and his voice dropped an octave, "I am coming for you, baby, with Atomic Rex right behind me. Keep me posted on where you and Yetaiju are. It's time to bring this plan of ours to a close and to see who the mightiest kaiju on the planet is!"

CHAPTER 25

BRAZIL

Kate was awakened by the sound of Yetaiju standing and sniffing the air. Kate looked up at the yeti, as she was surprised to see how well his wounds had healed. The deep wound on Yetaiju's shoulder had healed to the point that it was only half the size it had been before the monster had fallen asleep. Kate had seen Atomic Rex's incredible healing abilities, and while Yetaiju did not seem to heal as fast as the saurian creature, she was still impressed with how quickly the beast could recover from serious injuries.

Yetaiju shifted his head to the south and he sniffed the air again. The kaiju growled then bent down and scooped up Kate in his hand. Yetaiju lifted Kate roughly to his chest level then started walking in a southwest direction. Kate curled her body up around her radio to hide it as much as possible from Yetaiju's sight then whispered into it, "Chris, Yetaiju is heading in a southwest direction with me in his hand. He is constantly sniffing the air. I am pretty sure that he is following the scent of the displaced Peruvians."

Chris responded in a whisper, "Copy that. Atomic Rex has been following me more for the past several hours. I have a radar contact which I believe is you and Yetaiju. By my calculations, we should intercept you within the hour." Chris paused for a moment. "Kate, Steel Samurai 2.0 suffered major damage and I used up all of my ammunition in the battle with Liopleviathan. I can fly the robot, but I can't attack any of the kaiju."

Kate took a deep breath as she took in the information. "So unless the two monsters kill each other, we are going to be left with one of them."

Kate could hear the fear in Chris's voice as informed her of the other implications of the mech's damage. "It's not just that, Kate. I can't force Yetaiju to release you."

"He will put me down before he engages in a battle. Draw Atomic Rex to him then fly straight up. I will run in a straight line in the opposite direction of the two monsters. As soon as I am far enough away from them, fly down and pick me up. We will have to see how the battle plays itself out then decide how we will proceed from there."

Chris nodded. "Okay, Kate, I love you, and I can't wait to have you sitting next to me again."

Kate smiled as she looked at Yetaiju's hand. "I love you too, Chris. I have to warn you though, I might smell a little like a yeti when you see me." The two soulmates shared a brief laugh which helped to relieve the stress of the upcoming battle that would dictate the future of what remained of humanity.

The scent of the yeti-like creatures grew stronger with every step that Yetaiju took. The beast had no idea what he was going to do with the creatures when he found them. All that he knew was that he had an instinctual desire to surround himself with others like him, and these creatures appeared to be his best option to fit that role. Yetaiju was moving along at a very quick walk when he suddenly stopped and tilted his head in a northeast direction. The giant yeti's keen olfactory senses were picking up the scent of some other creature. Whatever the beast was, it had the same toxic sent to it that Armorsaur did. Yetaiju growled in the direction of the creature then turned and continued walking toward the fleeing Peruvians.

Kate was watching Yetaiju closely, and she was pretty sure she knew what the yeti had detected by his facial expressions. She grabbed her radio and whispered, "Chris, hurry. I think Yetaiju has detected Atomic Rex, but instead of running out to meet him, the yeti has decided to continue chasing the Peruvians. You may have to pick up the pace if we are going to have Atomic Rex intercept Yetaiju before he reaches the evacuees."

Chris responded with a quick, "Copy that. I'll see what I can do." With the current state of Steel Samurai 2.0, the mech was not able to reach anywhere near its top speed. Chris was flying the mech far above Atomic Rex in order to stay out of the kaiju's reach because the kaiju was easily keeping pace with Steel Samurai 2.0 at its current speed. Chris increased the mech's speed until the heavily damaged mech started to shake. Chris had only increased the mech's speed by about forty miles per hour, but it was enough for Atomic Rex to increase his speed in order to keep pace with the robot.

Twenty minutes after she had last spoken to her husband, Kate and Yetaiju had reached a long flat grassland area. They walked through the grassland for roughly ten minutes when Yetaiju suddenly came to a dead stop. The kaiju was staring out over the field at something, and when Kate looked in the same direction, she saw them. From this distance, they looked like tiny ants moving along the grassland, but the shapes were unmistakably human. Yetaiju had found the Peruvians. Kate was fully aware that even though the Peruvians seemed far away, in reality, the distance was only a short sprint away for Yetaiju. She grabbed her radio, "Chris, we have the Peruvians in sight. Where are you?"

The answer to Kate's question came in the form of an earth-shaking roar. Both Kate and Yetaiju's heads snapped in the direction of the roar. On the horizon to their left, they could see Steel Samurai 2.0 floating in the air with Atomic Rex below him.

Yetaiju returned the roar with a rage that rivaled that anger he felt when he encountered Armorsaur. The yeti had finally found his new family and was determined to prevent another kaiju from slaying them before his eyes. Yetaiju carefully placed Kate on the ground then sprinted toward Atomic Rex.

Kate ran off in the opposite direction of Yetaiju while Chris took Steel Samurai 2.0 to its maximum possible height. He then flew over the charging yeti and landed in front of the fleeing Kate. Kate immediately grabbed onto the exterior ladder of the mech and she began scaling it. When she reached the hatch on the mech's head, Chris threw it open and he leaned forward to kiss his wife. Kate quickly pushed his head back into the hatch. "Kiss me later. Right now, get us in the air and out of the reach of those monsters!"

Chris smiled then quickly complied with his wife's command.

When he reached Atomic Rex, Yetaiju struck the saurian kaiju with a blow that snapped his head to the left and rocked his entire body. The yeti quickly followed up with a blow from his left fist that snapped Atomic Rex's head back the other way. Atomic Rex took a half step back then sprang forward at Yetaiju. The nuclear theropod wrapped his powerful arms around Yetaiju's chest while at the same time slamming the top of his head into the primate's face.

Atomic Rex threw Yetaiju to the ground. He then bent down to tear out the yeti's throat. Yetaiju instinctively threw his left arm in front of his face to protect himself. Atomic Rex closed his jaws around the yeti's arm. The saurian kaiju's teeth sank deep into the yeti's arm, slicing through muscles and tissue before finally reaching bone. With his teeth latched onto Yetaiju's arm, Atomic Rex began to shake his head from side to side in an attempt to tear off the limb.

Yetaiju shrieked in pain as he delivered punch after punch to Atomic Rex's head, neck, and shoulder area. Each blow was capable of crushing a boulder and the barrage of punches caused Atomic Rex to release his grip on Yetaiju's arm.

With his arm badly bleeding, Yetaiju quickly shifted into a crouching position. He then leapt at Atomic Rex, wrapped his arms around the kaiju's mid-section, and tackled him to the ground. Yetaiju then climbed onto of Atomic Rex's chest where he began repeatedly striking the nuclear theropod in the face.

Chris and Kate were watching the battle from the cockpit of Steel Samurai 2.0. Kate looked over at Chris. "If Atomic Rex wins, have him follow us to the Atlantic Ocean; we can still salvage our plan to keep him in South America and to relocate the Peruvians."

Chris shook his head as Yetaiju continued to pound Atomic Rex's face into the ground. "What about if Yetaiju wins?"

Kate shook her head. "If he wins, I want you to fly next to him and set Steel Samurai 2.0's nuclear reactor to explode."

Chris looked at his wife. "That will kill the Peruvians as well."

Kate continued to keep her eyes fixed on the battle. "I know, but for the sake of our settlement and our kids, we can't let Yetaiju leave this field alive. Trust me; as far as the Peruvians go, giving them an instantaneous death will be the best thing we can do for them if Yetaiju wins this fight."

Atomic Rex was being bludgeoned into unconsciousness when he reached up with his claw and slashed it across Yetaiju's face, creating three deep gashes in the yeti's forehead, nose, and cheek. Yetaiju quickly reached up with both of his hands to cover his injured face. Having successfully halted the yeti's barrage, Atomic Rex placed his claws on Yetaiju's chest and he pushed the beast off him. Yetaiju tumbled to the ground and Atomic Rex regained his feet. Yetaiju was trying to stand when Atomic Rex spun his body around and sent his thick tail crashing into Yetaiju's face. The blow staggered the yeti and caused him to fall flat on his back.

Atomic Rex moved in to finish off his foe when Yetaiju again quickly shifted into a crouching position. This time, when the yeti leapt at Atomic Rex, he hooked his right arm under the kaiju's leg and he wrapped his left arm around the reptile's shoulder. Yetaiju then stood and lifted Atomic Rex off the ground. The yeti turned Atomic Rex over in his arms, and then he slammed the nuclear theropod to the ground, jarring every bone in the saurian creature's body.

Yetaiju threw out his arms and roared at the fallen Atomic Rex. Atomic Rex replied by rolling over and biting into Yetaiju's right thigh. Atomic Rex then stood and pulled on Yetaiju's leg, causing the yeti to fall onto his back. As soon as Yetaiju hit the ground, he kicked out with free leg, striking Atomic Rex in the throat and causing the saurian kaiju to release his grip.

Yetaiju stood and charged Atomic Rex. The yeti ducked under Atomic Rex's jaws then wrapped his powerful arms around the saurian creature's neck. Yetaiju strangled Atomic Rex while at the same time unleashing his freezing power on the nuclear theropod.

Atomic Rex was struggled to break Yetaiju's grip but not even he was able to overcome the yeti's awesome strength. Atomic Rex's lungs were yearning for air, and he could feel his scales freezing, cracking, and falling off his body. When he realized that he could not free himself of Yetaiju's freezing grip, Atomic Rex reached deep within his cells to unlock the nuclear power within them. Yetaiju's eyes shifted to Atomic Rex's body when he felt intense heat coming off the kaiju. The yeti saw a blue light forming beneath Atomic Rex's scales, and then he only saw a flash of blue as the skin was burned off nearly every inch of his body.

Yetaiju's own powerful grip caused him to catch the entire brunt of the Atomic Wave. Had the yeti simply been standing next to Atomic Rex, he would have been thrown by the blast, but because he was holding onto Atomic Rex, his body absorbed the full impact of the Atomic Wave. The blue dome of energy flowed out of Atomic Rex and through Yetaiju before slowly dissipating.

Yetaiju's arms slid off Atomic Rex and his body slumped to the ground. The front half of his body had no fur or skin left on it. The yeti's body was nothing but exposed muscles, and in some areas, bone. Yetaiju saw Atomic Rex standing above him. Yetaiju tried to stand and continue the battle, but the damage to his body was too severe. All the yeti could do was turn his head. His head lolled to the side and he looked over at the fleeing Peruvians in the distance. The yeti tried to reach for his new family, but all that he could manage to do was stretch his fingers out toward them. He was still looking at the Peruvians as Atomic Rex bent over and closed his jaws on Yetaiju's head and shoulders. The nuclear theropod shook Yetaiju's head until he felt the primate's neck snap. With the most powerful adversary he had every faced vanquished before him, Atomic Rex placed his foot on Yetaiju's corpse. The saurian kaiju then roared, alerting every living creature in the area of his victory. Atomic Rex shifted his eyes to the dead Yetaiju, and then he bent down and began eating the yeti.

Kate breathed a sigh of relief. "Thank God." She looked toward Chris. "We can take steps to meet Atomic Rex's needs and keep him away from us. Yetaiju would have stalked us across the continent and beyond to find a sense of belonging that we couldn't provide."

She looked over at Chris. "Okay, now fly by him and start having him follow us toward the Atlantic Ocean. When we are roughly one hundred miles from the east coast of Brazil, take us as high as the robot can go so that we are out of Atomic Rex's sight."

Chris was just staring at Atomic Rex as he devoured the remains of Yetaiju. Kate leaned over to her husband, "What are you waiting for? Get the monster's attention and start luring him away from here before he goes after the Peruvians!"

Chris looked at his wife. "You said I could kiss you later." He smiled. "I don't care about the yeti smell."

Kate leaned over and gave her husband a quick kiss on the check. "It's a long flight home. After we ditch Atomic Rex, and if the autopilot still works, there is a lot more in store for you where that came from."

Chris smiled. "If it doesn't work I'll find a way to make it work." He then flew Steel Samurai 2.0 in a circle around Atomic Rex. The kaiju roared at the hated mech then lunged at it. Chris increased the mech's altitude above Atomic Rex's range to reach them. He then set a course for the Atlantic Ocean. Atomic Rex left the slain yeti behind and he took off after the fleeing mech.

As they were flying away, Kate grabbed the radio. "Emily, Kyle, come in."

She held the radio for a few moments before she heard her son's voice, "Mom! It's Kyle! Are you okay?"

She smiled. "I am fine. I am with Dad inside Steel Samurai 2.0. Yetaiju is dead and Atomic Rex is following us toward the east coast of South America. Listen carefully; I need you and Emily to work with the boat captains. We need the boats gassed up and then we need them to head to the coast of southern Peru. I will send you exact coordinates later. Dad and I are going to keep leading Atomic Rex away from the survivors from the Peruvian camp. I will radio their leader and have him take his people to the coast where the boats can pick them up. The boats are then to take the survivors to southern Mexico where we will help them start a new camp."

Kyle replied, "Okay, Mom, were are on it."

Kate then called General Mendoza. "General Mendoza, we are leading Atomic Rex away from your group. Have your people head to the coast; we will have boats meet you there. They will take you to Mexico where we will help you to establish a new campsite."

Mendoza replied with a reverence in his voice, "Thank you."

Kate then put down the radio and she and Chris looked at Atomic Rex as the monster continued to follow them into the interior of Brazil.

EPILOGUE

SIX MONTHS AFTER THE DEATH OF YETAIJU

After losing Atomic Rex in the interior of Brazil, Chris and Kate flew back to North America where they used Steel Samurai 2.0 to pick up the nuclear reactors they had placed around the Great Lakes to help keep Atomic Rex there. They placed one of the reactors in Brazil and the other two in southern Colombia and Venezuela. Kate hoped that by placing the reactors there, and with the abundance of giant mutants in South America, that Atomic Rex would not have to enter North America in order to feed or absorb energy.

In southern Mexico, people from Kate's camp were able to help the Peruvians set up a new campsite with sustainable fishing and farming operations to supply food for them. They were also able to dig wells to supply drinking water for the population.

In Washington, the engineers were able to help Chris repair Steel Samurai 2.0 to the point where the mech would still be able to function well enough to be utilized as a fishing vehicle and a desalination mechanism.

The former council leaders met with Kate and they agreed to step down from their positions. They formerly apologized for their attempts to undermine her and they helped her organize elections that would form a new council. Many of the people in the settlement suggested the Emily should be a part of the new council, but the young woman declined the position stating that she preferred to continue to be in charge of tracking Ramrod and studying his habits.

She also proved her valor by formerly introducing Sean to her father as her boyfriend. Chris quickly pulled Sean aside and informed him of what was and was not acceptable in regards to a boyfriend's actions in regards to his daughter. Sean quickly agreed to all of Chris's terms.

Kyle accepted an official position as advisor to his mother where he could learn from her and sharpen the skills that would help him assume a leadership position in the campsite as he matured.

Deep in the Amazon Rainforest, a giant mutant jaguar was walking along the river hunting for food. The creature came to the edge of the water and he stared down into it in search of giant fish or reptiles. The jaguar heard a pounding sound like thunder from the jungle. The jaguar felt the ground shaking beneath his paws and he heard a roar split the sky. The jaguar looked across the river to see the awesome form of Atomic Rex staring at him. Atomic Rex roared at the jaguar then sprinted toward the feline.

THE END

CHECK OUT OTHER GREAT
KAIJU NOVELS

KAIJU WINTER
by Jake Bible

The Yellowstone super volcano has begun to erupt, sending North America into chaos and the rest of the world into panic. People are dangerous and desperate to escape the oncoming mega-eruption, knowing it will plunge the continent, and the world, into a perpetual ashen winter. But no matter how ready humanity is, nothing can prepare them for what comes out of the ash: Kaiju!

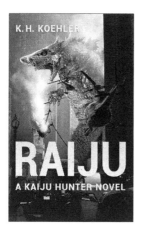

RAIJU
by K.H. Koehler

His home destroyed by a rampaging kaiju, Kevin Takahashi and his father relocate to New York City where Kevin hopes the nightmare is over. Soon after his arrival in the Big Apple, a new kaiju emerges. Qilin is so powerful that even the U.S. Military may be unable to contain or destroy the monster. But Kevin is more than a ragged refugee from the now defunct city of San Francisco. He's also a Keeper who can summon ancient, demonic god-beasts to do battle for him, and his creature to call is Raiju, the oldest of the ancient Kami. Kevin has only a short time to save the city of New York. Because Raiju and Qilin are about to clash, and after the dust settles, there may be no home left for any of them!

CHECK OUT OTHER GREAT
KAIJU NOVELS

MURDER WORLD | KAIJU DAWN
by Jason Cordova
& Eric S Brown

Captain Vincente Huerta and the crew of the Fancy have been hired to retrieve a valuable item from a downed research vessel at the edge of the enemy's space.
It was going to be an easy payday.
But what Captain Huerta and the men, women and alien under his command didn't know was that they were being sent to the most dangerous planet in the galaxy.
Something large, ancient and most assuredly evil resides on the planet of Gorgon IV. Something so terrifying that man could barely fathom it with his puny mind. Captain Huerta must use every trick in the book, and possibly write an entirely new one, if he wants to escape Murder World.

KAIJU ARMAGEDDON
by Eric S. Brown

The attacks began without warning. Civilian and Military vessels alike simply vanished upon the waves. Crypto-zoologist Jerry Bryson found himself swept up into the chaos as the world discovered that the legendary beasts known as Kaiju are very real. Armies of the great beasts arose from the oceans and burrowed their way free of the Earth to declare war upon mankind. Now Dr. Bryson may be the human race's last hope in stopping the Kaiju from bringing civilization to its knees.
This is not some far distant future. This is not some alien world. This is the Earth, here and now, as we know it today, faced with the greatest threat its ever known. The Kaiju Armageddon has begun.

CHECK OUT OTHER GREAT
KAIJU NOVELS

KAIJU SPAWN
by David Robbins
& Eric S Brown

Wally didn't believe it was really the end of the world until he saw the Kaiju with his own eyes. The great beasts rose from the Earth's oceans, laying waste to civilization. Now Wally must fight his way across the Kaiju ravaged wasteland of modern day America in search of his daughter. He is the only hope she has left . . . and the clock is ticking.

From authors David Robbins (Endworld) and Eric S Brown (Kaiju Apocalypse), Kaiju Spawn is an action packed, horror tale of desperate determination and the battle to overcome impossible odds.

KUA MAU
by Mark Onspaugh

The Spider Islands. A mysterious ship has completed a treacherous journey to this hidden island chain. Their mission: to capture the legendary monster, Kua'Mau. Thinking they are successful, they sail back to the United States, where the terrifying creature will be displayed at a new luxury casino in Las Vegas. But the crew has made a horrible mistake - they did not trap Kua'Mau, they took her offspring. Now hot on their heels comes a living nightmare, a two hundred foot, one hundred ton tentacled horror, Kua'Mau, Kaiju Mother of Wrath, who will stop at nothing to safeguard her young. As she tears across California heading towards Vegas, she leaves a monumental body-count in her wake, and not even the U.S. military or private black ops can stop this city-crushing, havoc-wreaking monstrous mother of all Kaiju as she seeks her revenge.

CHECK OUT OTHER GREAT KAIJU NOVELS

ATOMIC REX
by Matthew Dennion

The war is over, humanity has lost, and the Kaiju rule the earth.

Three years have passed since the US government attempted to use giant mechs to fight off an incursion of kaiju. The eight most powerful kaiju have carved up North America into their respective territories and their mutant offspring also roam the continent. The remnants of humanity are gathered in a remote settlement with Steel Samurai, the last of the remaining mechs, as their only protection. The mech is piloted by Captain Chris Myers who realizes that humanity will not survive if they stay at the settlement. In order to preserve the human race, he leaves the settlement unprotected as he engages on a desperate plan to draw the eight kaiju into each other's territories. His hope is that the kaiju will destroy each other. Chris will encounter horrors including the amorphous Amebos, Tortiraus the Giant turtle , and the nuclear powered mutant dinosaur Atomic Rex!

KAIJU DEADFALL
by JE Gurley

Death from space. The first meteor landed in the Pacific Ocean near San Francisco, causing an earthquake and a tsunami. The second wiped out a small Indiana city. The third struck the deserts of Nevada. When gigantic monsters- Ishom, Girra, and Nusku- emerge from the impact craters, the world faces a threat unlike any it had ever known - Kaiju . NASA catastrophist Gate Rutherford and Special Ops Captain Aiden Walker must find a way to stop the creatures before they destroy every major city in America..

23916586R00112

Printed in Great Britain
by Amazon